MW01488190

History Is Fascinating—
And I Can Prove It!

Other Vantage Press titles by this author:

Little Suggestion Book for College Students (2005)
Wit and Wisdom for Senior Citizens (2006)

History Is Fascinating —And I Can Prove It!

Homer J. Adams

VANTAGE PRESS
New York

Cover design by Susan Thomas

FIRST EDITION

All rights reserved, including the right of
reproduction in whole or in part in any form.

Copyright © 2008 by Homer J. Adams

Published by Vantage Press, Inc.
419 Park Ave. South, New York, NY 10016

Manufactured in the United States of America
ISBN: 978-0-533-15881-2

Library of Congress Catalog Card No.: 2007933738

0 9 8 7 6 5 4 3 2 1

To students in my history classes across the years

Contents

III. The Nineteenth Century

Preface

People don't automatically like history but they love a good story. They also like anything that makes them laugh. History is a story or rather, a collection of stories about people, and how they lived and loved. These accounts are shot through and through with humor and human interest, which, for too long, has been minimized in the study of history.

Political regimes, dynasties, and wars are important but recognizing the human interest involved in those facts provides seasoning to make them palatable.

These stories are designed for those who already have a fondness for history, for the man on the street (and woman) who has an open mind toward learning more about the past, and for students who will enroll in a history course.

May these accounts, ranging from Eratosthenes to Katrina, increase the number of people who reach for a book on history for recreational reading.

Introduction

The articles and stories that follow, while meeting the definition of history, are rich in anecdotes and other human interest materials. Herodotus, "the father of history," in the 5th century B.C., included anecdotes in his writings. He may have relied too much on eye-witnesses for some of his stories are not credible.

Brief stories couched in the simple language of the listeners, formed a vital part in the teachings of Jesus. These parables beginning with understandable phrases as, "Behold a sower went forth to sow," and "A certain man had two sons," caught and held the attention of the listeners. People still like new information to be related to their lives. Human nature and reactions are much the same across the centuries.

People, old and young, are fascinated by an interesting story. Peter Jennings, interviewed on ABC in 2005, spoke of his audience and said, "You can always get them with a good story." Someone said that a good story can "draw old men from their chimney corners and children from their play."

People react much the same across the centuries. I have heard two jokes in my lifetime, which were being told, with slightly different detail, 2000 years ago. What was funny then still "tickles people's funny bone" today.

The purpose of the human interest emphasis is to inject into the study of history the vividness and sparkle present at the time of the event being described. Too often this is filtered out. History does not have to be dull to be accurate. Theodore Roosevelt was aware of this need when, in an address to the American Historical Association in 1912, he made this plea to historians:

> He must ever remember that while the worst offense of which he can be guilty is to write vividly and inaccurately, yet, that unless, he writes vividly he cannot write truthfully; for no amount of dull, painstaking detail will sum up the whole truth unless the genius is there to paint the truth.[1]

Samuel Eliot Morison commented that this appeal fell on deaf ears and he went on to complain of "a sort of chain reaction of dullness in history writing."[2] This certainly does not describe his writing, for his masterpiece biography of Columbus, *Admiral of the Ocean Sea*, is rich in interesting detail.

Some anecdotes are based on truth though not technically true. Let me explain. There is reason to doubt Parson Weems' account of little George Washington cutting down the cherry tree, to which he confessed by saying "I cannot tell a lie; I did it with my little hatchet." This portrayed an American hero who did not lie, which was typical of him. It was an accurate portrayal and his contemporaries, who knew him best, believed it.

History is defined as "a record of past events and persons, written as fairly and accurately as the writer knows how to do." I believe these stories measure up to this criterion.

Those of us who want Americans, young and old, to appreciate and read history will hope they consider G.M. Trevelyan's statement:

> How wonderful a thing it is to look back into the past as it actually was, to get a glimpse through the curtain of old night into some brilliantly lighted scene of living men and women, not mere creatures of fiction and imagination, but warm-blooded realities even as we are.[3]

History is fascinating and humor, anecdotes, and other human interest material can be skillfully inserted to season the account of past events and make them palatable. History should be presented so interestingly that people would pull such a book off the shelf for casual reading.

[1] Roosevelt, Theodore, "History as Literature" *American Historical Review*, XVIII, 1912–1913, 473–89.
[2] Morison, Samuel Eliot, "History as a Literary Art," *Old South Leaflets*, Series II, No. 1 (Boston: The Old South Association) p. 4.
[3] Trevelyan, G. M., *History and the Reader*, London, Cambridge University Press, 1945.

History Is Fascinating—
And I Can Prove It!

I

World History

Measuring the Earth

Eratosthenes, a Greek living in Alexandria, Egypt in the 3rd century B.C., measured the size of the earth with amazing accuracy. Columbus thought it was much smaller and when he discovered the New World, he was convinced he had arrived at China. He carried with him, for years, letters addressed to the great Khan, from Queen Isabella.

Eratosthenes learned that the sun, at its northernmost point, shone straight down to the bottom of a well at the first cataract of the Nile. He set up his instruments at Alexandria, 500 miles away, and measured the sun at its zenith there, as well as the sun above the other site. He discovered that the angle between the sun, at the two points was 7 1/5 degrees, or 1/50th of the 360 degrees of the earth's circumference. He assumed the two points were on the same meridian and computed that the distance around the earth was a few hundred less than the 25,000 miles of the total circumference of the earth. He figured its diameter at 7,850 miles which is within 50 miles of being correct.[1]

1

What a shame that geographers and explorers in the 15th century did not read ancient history!

With modern technology measurements can be made with amazing accuracy. Celestial navigation—"shooting" the sun or stars, and working through intricate tables, in HO 211 and HO 214, taught in naval midshipman school, is a thing of the past. No longer does an officer stand on a heaving deck, trying to hold the sextant steady, while he measures the altitude and bearing of a heavenly body. Rather, he presses a button and G.P.S. tells him where he is.

[1] Breasted, James Henry, *Ancient Times*, Revised edition, Boston, Ginn, 1963.

Nero in Life and Death

The Roman Emperor, Nero, is usually remembered for his persecution of Christians, and the legend that he "fiddled while Rome burned." He saw himself as a musician, athlete, and actor. In Greece, in the year 66, he entered the chariot race, was thrown from the car and didn't finish the race. The judges however, knew an Emperor when they saw one, and awarded him the crown of victory.

When he performed in a theatre Suetonius said, "No one was allowed to leave, even for the most urgent reasons." Some women gave birth there, and others acted like they were dead, so as to be carried out.[1]

Then he was beset by foes, at home and abroad. The senate proclaimed General Alba, Emperor. His guard deserted him, and he fled from Rome, alone. He went to the Tiber to drown himself, but lost his nerve. He found refuge in Phaon's cellar, and spent a sleepless night. The word came that the senate had declared him a public enemy, and would have him put to death.

He determined to end his life. He took a poniard, put it to his throat, and cried "What an artist dies in me." But he faltered, and his freedman helped him press the blade home.[2]

Perhaps he said, like Vespasian, "Woe is me. I think I am about to become a god."

[1] Suetonius, *The Lives of the Twelve Caesars*, New York, Heritage Press, 1965.
[2] Durant, Will, Durant, Ariel, *Caesar and Christ*, v III, *The Story of Civilization*. New York, Simon and Schuster, 1967.

Historical Snapshots

There are many episodes in history that make a significant point and help us understand that chapter of the past. A brief account of these events is called a "historical snapshot." Some of these accounts are footnoted; others I learned from sources I deemed credible at the time but did not record details.

Diogenes and Alexander

Diogenes was a Greek philosopher living in the 4th century B.C. Legend has it that he walked the streets of Athens at midday carrying a lighted lantern. He was making a point. When asked why, he would reply that he was looking for an honest man.

Exponent of asceticism, he lived in a small hut on the hillside outside the city. Alexander the Great, wishing to honor the famous philosopher, came to visit him. The old man was reading a manuscript by the light streaming through the open door. Alexander stopped in the door, greeted him, and asked, "Is there anything I can do for you?" The response was, "Yes, get out of my light so I can see to read."

Gazette

The word Gazette is a popular name for a newspaper and it has an interesting origin. Newsletters were put out by the Venetian government in the 16th Century. They were read out loud in public places. People who wanted to hear the news had to pay one gazetta, a small Italian coin. Thus the name, Gazette a source of news.

Haircut in Silence

Barbers have been talking a lot for thousands of years. One ancient writer said this, "The barber has his shop, which is a center of the local gossips and gadflys." Another barber asked King Archelaus of Macedon how he would like his hair cut. The king must have known about garrulous barbers for he snapped "In silence."[1]

I was in Jacobs and Shearrin's barber shop on Murfreesboro Road in Nashville, years ago. This shop was a friendly place, tempting one to drop in even when a haircut was not needed just to hear arguments, related to the rural south, such as how to prepare "chitlins." Mr. Jake favored the "hand-flung," over the "stump-whipped" method, which he declared, bruised them.

One day I was waiting my turn when a middle-aged man advanced to an empty chair. The barber asked,

"What would you like?" The short answer was, "A medium trim, and mighty little conversation." I thought of the Macedonian barber from the sixth century. Across the centuries, the question and the answer were much the same.[1]

I read about one barber who talked so incessantly that he lost job after job. Then he went to Washington to cut hair in the Congressional barber shop in one of the House office buildings. His volubility was as strong as ever and the waiting ear in front of him was irresistible. He talked, as usual, but no one minded. Members of Congress were so used to hot air, that they paid no attention. His job was safe.

[1] Durant, Will and Ariel, *The Story of Civilization*, V.2, The Life of Greece, New York, Simon and Schuster, 1967.

Medieval Student Government

Some interesting stories come out of the Medieval Period, concerning higher education. There was a conflict between "town and gown", which became physical on occasion. The dominance of students over faculty, for a time, stands in sharp contrast with the present. The teachers were dependent on the fees paid them by the students. The "University of Students" bargained with the doctors (teachers), and the result was a set of regulations the doctors were bound to obey. They fixed salaries, the hours of instruction, and the number of lectures. If a doctor planned to be absent, he had to get the consent of the class and of the student-rector. If he wanted to leave town, he had to deposit some money as a pledge of intent to return. The professor had to begin class with a bell, and end the session one minute after the bell. The doctors were fined for leaving out material, or for refusing to answer questions. A committee of students visited classrooms to detect any irregularities.

Things changed when the doctors organized, forming a "University of Doctors." They set up a monopoly of the right to teach, to set examinations, and grant licenses. These were the earliest degrees.

I know of one university where students still wear gowns to class—the University of The South, Sewanee, Tennessee.

Ault, Warren O., *Europe in the Middle Ages*, Boston, D.C. Heath, 1937.

Advances in Science in the 1600s

Scientific study goes back as far as written history, and continued even in the Dark Ages and Middle Ages. The discovery of major laws of science characterized the seventeenth century in Europe. Learned societies in England and France were publishing scientific journals by the 1660s.

Galileo

Copernicus had advanced the revolutionary, heliocentric theory of the solar system in the 16th century, but it was left to Galileo in 1632, using the newly developed telescope, to confirm the Copernican theory. To hold that the earth moves around the sun shocked church leaders who had long held that the earth was the center of the universe. Galileo was hauled before a church court, and under the threat of death, commanded to recant his view that the earth orbited around the sun. He was a practical man, desiring to continue his scientific study, so he said "I recant." However, as he walked away, passing students and colleagues observing the trial, he said, in a stage whisper, "It is true, nonetheless." He was not totally silenced. His ideas lived on in his printed works.

Descartes Slept on His Back

A leading intellectual, in the 1660s, René Descartes was a philosopher and a mathematician. The Cartesian Method, named for him, emphasized stating a premise which seemed rationally acceptable, and then making deductions from it. Those in the next century, the age of enlightenment, found flaws in his method of doubt and examination of traditions by reason. He is also known for his quote, "I think, therefore I am."

To my regret, he invented analytic geometry, the toughest course I ever took. He was prone to sleep late, and while lying on his back in bed, he studied the ceiling tiles overhead. He saw where they joined at right angles, the x and y axes. From this he projected the ability to calculate the slope of a line, and the whole system of analytics. His "Cartesian Coordinates" were mysterious to me. I think he got de cart before de horse!

Brinton, Crane, Christopher, John B., Wolfe, Robert Lee, *Civilization in the West*, Englewood Cliffs, Prentice-Hall, 1964.
Lectures in "History of Ideas," George Peabody graduate school.

Martin Luther and the Protestant Revolt

Luther's search for salvation began in 1505 when he began to ask himself "When will you ever become pious and do enough to get a gracious God." He was convinced that salvation was by works. Several things happened that year to spur his anxious pursuit of spiritual peace: a close friend died, he stumbled and fell on his sword, wounding himself, and he had a close call during an electrical storm. Lightning struck nearby and he cried out, "Oh Saint Anna, I will become a priest." To him this was the way to success in his spiritual quest.

Luther was born in Eisleben, in Saxony, Germany in 1483. His father was a miner and he grew up in grinding poverty. He endured strict discipline with many floggings at home and at school and this made a lasting impression on him. He was steeped in the superstitions of his culture. Demons and devils seemed very real to him and this view followed him all through his life. His great hymn, "A Mighty Fortress" includes references to Satan and his power. The Devil was so real to Luther, in the castle at Wartburg, that he threw a bottle of ink at him.

In 1497 Luther went away to Magdeburg, to a school operated by mystics, The Brethren of the Common Life. Later in life he became a mystic. After this he went to an excellent school in Eisenach, where he earned part of his expenses singing in the church choir and serenading homes.

Luther became a novice in the Augustinian Monastery. He was a model monk, accepting menial duties assigned to him and asking for more. He believed in the sacrament of Penance and went so often that he made a nuisance of himself. There was still no peace. Then an older monk took an interest in him and directed him to the book of Romans. While reading Scripture his eyes fell on Romans 1:17 "The just shall live by faith." A light broke through and he was converted when he saw that it was by faith in God's grace and not by works that salvation was assured. This doctrine of "Justification by Faith" became the motto of the Protestant Reformation.

Luther was ordained a priest in 1507. Then his superiors decided he should be a teacher so he went to the new university at Wittenberg. While there he studied at Erfurt, earning his doctorate in 1512. In the year 1510–11 he went to Rome on church business and was disillusioned with the worldliness there.

Now came the beginning of the break with Rome. The church taught that the Pope could draw on the treasury of merit, surplus good works, left by the saints, to cancel punishment imposed in the sacrament of Penance, for the living and the dead. This "indulgence" could be purchased to get a loved one out of Purgatory.

A man named Tetzel came to a town near Wittenberg, with a papal bull (official letter), giving him the right to sell indulgences. He did a brisk business, chanting "As the coin dropped into the chest rings, a soul from Purgatory springs."

Luther was a parish priest as well as a teacher, and some of his flock was lured into this by Tetzel. His response was to post on the church door at Wittenberg in October, 1517, his "95 theses," that is, topics for discussion. These included strong attacks on the abuses of the indulgences. They included:

Every Christian, truly repentant, has full remission of guilt even without letter of pardon.
Why does not the Pope empty purgatory out of charity of heart?

News spread like wildfire. A professor named John Eck, attacked the theses as heresy. By 1518 the news reached Rome. Pope Leo X first said, "This is clever" but later changed to "These are the writings of a drunken monk."

Next he had the Curia warn Luther. When this official voice failed, he ordered Luther to Rome but the Elector of Saxony would not let him go, fearing for his life. Then the Pope sent Cardinal Cajetan to deal with the problem. He ordered Luther to recant. Luther defied the Legate, and the two angry men parted. Luther decided that the Pope was not the final authority and appealed his case to a general church council.

In 1520 the Pope issued a bull threatening excommunication if Luther did not recant. Then in 1521, the newly elected Holy Roman Emperor, Charles V, called a meeting, the Diet of Worms, to deal with Luther. Luther was called upon to recant by the electors, princes, Emperor, and Aleander, the Pope's representative. He refused, saying "Here I stand; unless I am clearly convinced by Scripture, I cannot and will not recant." By holding that popes and councils err, he denied the bases on which the church rests. This was considered rank heresy and he was placed under the ban of empire, outlaw status. A surging tide of German nationalism formed a background of the doctrinal dispute.

Luther's friends kidnapped him for his own safety and kept him in the castle at Wartburg. While there for ten months he translated the New Testament into German.

Lutheranism triumphed in Germany in the 1520s and it was impossible to enforce the imperial ban. In 1526 the German princes decided that each prince would decide which religion would be practiced—Catholic or Lutheran. Luther guided the new movement, working out a new ritual of worship and a catechism.

In 1529 Charles V announced that armed force would be used and called the Diet of Spires. The German princes issued a "protest," the source of the word "Protestant." He tried again in the 1530s, 1540s, and 1550s to impose his will on Germany. He failed, resigned and retreated to a monastery in 1555, collected a room full of clocks and vainly tried to get them all to tick at once.

The results of the Lutheran revolt, and other reform efforts, are clearly seen in the Protestant and Catholic Church worlds today.

Lucas, Henry S., *The Renaissance and the Reformation*, New York, Harper and Row, 1960, Second Edition.
Lectures by Dr. Batten, Vanderbilt Professor, in the course, "Renaissance and Reformation."
Note: The term "Holy Roman Empire," whose power was rated so highly by Charles V, was more of a loose confederation. Someone observed that "It was neither holy nor Roman nor empire." It took Charles V a long time to admit its ineffectiveness.

Brief Glimpses of Renaissance Scholars

Francesco Petrarch (1304–1374)
Petrarch was said to be the first man in 1,000 years to climb a mountain just to see the sun rise. This Renaissance leader and classic scholar was running counter to the view in the medieval period that the beauty of the earth was to be abhorred. Petrarch enjoyed the view but tradition compelled him to sit down and read from a book before he descended.

The rebirth of learning in the 13th century and the two that followed influenced painting, sculpture, music, philosophy, science, and the church. It was the era of the "greats"—Dante, DaVinci, Raphael, Michelangelo, and many more. The humanists were said to be the midwives of the new renaissance culture. It was a revolt against medieval thought and a renewed interest in the Greek and Roman classics.

Petrarch got carried away with his fascination with the works of Cicero. In a meeting with other scholars, Petrarch heard one of them criticize the great one. He quickly reproved his fellow scholar, saying, "Gently, gently with my Cicero." Dr. Batten, Vanderbilt professor, said that Petrarch reluctantly loaned a Cicero manuscript to a friend and then soon began to remind him to return it.

Archbishop Laud

Formerly chancellor at Oxford, where he counted the spoons after his induction feast, Laud led the English high church group in bitter conflict with the Puritans in the 1620s and 1630s. In this period one's religious views also indicated a political and social attitude. He and his group were in full power and were harassing the nonconformists. They had the backing of Charles I. Earlier the King had said, "They will conform or I will harry them out of the land." One Puritan preacher, taking note of the Archbishop's small stature, proclaimed from the pulpit, "All glory to God and little laud to the Devil." The surging power of Puritans and gentry focused their displeasure on Laud. Six hundred apprentices picketed his palace at Lambeth and he retreated to Whitehall, protected by the "royal guards." His fortunes declined, as did those of Charles I, ousted by the Puritan parliament, and put to death in 1649. Laud was executed in 1645. Puritanism prevailed, for a time and then royal rule was restored in 1660.

Lectures in a "Renaissance and Reformation" course taught by Dr. Batten, Vanderbilt Professor.
Lucas, Henry S., *The Renaissance and the Reformation*, Second Edition, New York, Harper and Row, 1960.

Columbus and the Moon's Eclipse

On Columbus' fourth voyage, misfortune overtook him. About half his men led by the Porras brothers, mutinied and deserted, leaving him sick and marooned at Santa Gloria in Jamaica. He was also short of food and faced hostile Tainos Indians who were resisting bringing more food to barter with the Spanish ships.

Then he had a bright idea. He consulted a book, *Ephemerides*, printed at Nuremberg in the previous century, which predicted eclipses. In three days time, on February 29, 1504, a total eclipse of the moon was predicted, so the Admiral called a conference of Indian chiefs and they met aboard the *Capitana* on February 29.

Columbus made a speech in which he said Christians worshipped the God of Heaven who rewarded the good and punished the bad. He disapproved of the rebellion and the failure of the Indians to bring food. They would be punished with famine and pestilence and would soon receive a token from Heaven, an inflamed and bloody moon. This would signal punishment to come. The Indians departed, some in fear and some scoffing. Then when the moon began to rise, red in color, and then beginning the eclipse, the natives began to howl and mourn, and run to the ships laden with provisions. They pled with the Admiral to intercede for them and promised to supply all that was needed in the future.

Columbus promised to consult with God, and then retired, and remained while the eclipse lasted. As the eclipse ended he came forth from his cabin, reported that their pleas had been heard and that they were forgiven as long as they treated the Christians well. Even as he spoke the eclipse ended, and the natives began to thank him and praise his God.[1]

The Spaniards found another way to get food by using fishhounds. The Indians captured pilot fish, the type with a sucker on the top of its head, used to attach to a shark, tamed them and used them to hunt fish and turtles. They would fasten a fiber string to one's tail, point it to its prey and pay out the line. The pilot fish would attach itself to a turtle and would be brought in by the use of a crude reel. Four turtles were caught as the Spaniards watched, and were given to them for food.[2]

I can attest to the suction power of these fish. We caught big ones in the South Pacific in W.W. II. If one rolled over and clamped onto the wooden deck, it took great strength to dislodge it.

[1] Morison, Samuel Eliot, *Admiral of the Ocean Sea*, Boston, Little, Brown and Co., 1942, II.
[2] Ibid.

Queen Elizabeth's Toothache

Elizabeth I, daughter of Henry VIII and Anne Boleyn, ruled England from 1558 to 1603. She was spirited and courageous and she needed to be, for pressures on her were great and her life was in danger.

Churchill said that she had "a commanding carriage, auburn hair, eloquence of speech and natural dignity."[1]

In her latter years she was prone to see enemies where they weren't and would walk down the long halls of the palace thrusting her sword into the draperies in case anyone was hiding there.

She knew trauma early because her father, Henry VIII, had her mother executed. Anne did not bear him a male child. She also knew that the Duke of Northumberland, who dominated Edward VI, and Lady Jane Grey, proclaimed Queen in 1554, were both executed at the block. She had lived through the persecution of Protestants by Mary Tudor, and instituted her own execution of Catholic priests in the 1570s and 1580s. She succeeded her half-sister Mary Tudor, at the age of twenty-five. She could deal with matters of life and death better than she could a physical ailment.[2]

Queen Elizabeth I developed a toothache one October, and her plight distressed her courtiers, who mourned over her pain. A brave woman in other regards, she shrank from doing anything about it. It came to a climax when the pain became unbearable. She was unable to sleep for forty-eight hours.

A special meeting of the Privy Council was called to discuss the matter. They were dealing with a forty-five-year-old woman who had never had a tooth pulled, and was refusing to have it done. The council voted unanimously for tooth extraction. A group of them took a surgeon, and went to see the suffering Queen.

One of them was Bishop John Alymer, a lifelong admirer. The Council's view was reported to the Queen, and before she could protest, Alymer told her that his teeth were at her service. He volunteered to have one of his teeth extracted to show that it was no great matter. The surgeon then pulled one of the bishop's teeth, after which she agreed to have her own extracted.[3]

[1] Churchill, Winston, *The New World*, New York, Dodd, Mead and Company, 1956.
[2] Smith, Goldwin, *A History of England*, New York, Charles Scribner's sons, 1966, Third Edition.
[3] Jenkins, Elizabeth, *Elizabeth the Great*, New York. Coward McCann, 1960.

Marie Antoinette and Husband

This Queen was the unpopular wife of Louis XVI, King of France. As a ruler he was ineffective, wishy-washy, yet stubborn. He seemed unaware, or at least not capable of understanding, the smoldering resentment of the French people over the terrible abuse they had suffered. An intolerably heavy burden, of taxes, fell upon the poor people and were avoided by the upper classes. Those led to the French Revolution in 1789, perhaps the bloodiest in the history of the world.

When the populace were protesting in the streets, and demanding bread, Marie Antoinette is quoted as saying "If they have no bread, let them eat cake." Historians doubt that she really said this, but the people believed that she did. The libel has stuck for two centuries.

The French national assembly, the Convention, abolished the monarchy and declared France to be a republic. The reign of terror began, and in 1793 Louis XVI was tried and executed. Marie followed, and on the way to the guillotine she trod on the toe of the executioner. She said "Pardon, Monsieur," her last words. After executing royalty, leaders began to turn on one another, and the "national razor" was kept busy. Truly, "A revolution devours its children."

The little son of Louis XVI and Marie Antoinette, the Dauphin, mysteriously disappeared. He was rumored to have emigrated to New Orleans, Louisiana and several pretenders appeared, claiming to be the lost Dauphin or a descendant.

The Captain of the ship I served in, during World War II, was named LaBonte, and his ancestor claimed to be the lost prince. I was the Executive Officer, and when I reported the crew's dissatisfaction with the food, he flung out his arm and said, "As my great, great, great grandmother said, "Let them eat cake." I'm afraid I didn't follow through with his suggestion. Sailors always gripe about the food. The men on our sub-chaser had better rations than most, as we had a creative cook. He served hot pecan rolls on Sunday morning, along with baked beans and cornbread.

Gershoy, Leo, *The French Revolution and Napoleon*, Appleton-Century-Crofts, New York, 1964.

II

Seventeenth and Eighteenth Centuries

Indian Corn and a Deer Trap

On November 20, 1620, with a patent to locate in Virginia, the Pilgrims sighted the shore of Cape Cod. While still aboard the *Mayflower* they had written and signed the "Mayflower Compact," an agreement to form a political group responsible to the will of the majority. This replaced the now useless Virginia patent.

Upon landing, they faced the problem of learning about the strange land and of finding food. On the following Monday Captain Miles Standish, William Bradford, and two others went exploring. They found corn, cleverly buried in baskets, which they took "to be repaid later." Returning home they came across an Indian snare to catch deer, a small tree, bent over, fastened with a home-made rope with a loop, near acorns scattered around. Bradford was examining the trap when it caught his leg and jerked him into the air. Imagine the future governor, hoisted upside down, and calling for help.[1]

I don't believe Bradford records this indignity in his *Historie*.

Indians not only provided corn for the starving settlers, they taught them how to raise it. One technique was to put a fish in each hill, for fertilizer.

[1] Howe, Henry F., *Prologue to New England*, New York, Farrar and Rhinehart, 1943.

Life in the Colonies in the 1700s

The Paper Shroud of Jonathan Edwards

The mid-1700s saw, in the American colonies, a religious revival, known as the "Great Awakening". The powerful exhortations of Jonathan Edwards on such subjects as "Punishment of the Wicked" had a great influence on the start of this revival. While a child he was precociously interested in salvation and built a hut in the woods where he could pray. His ten sisters said he prayed five times a day.

In college he would go deep into the woods to meditate and pray. In mental agitation, he would make notes and pin them to his greatcoat. When he emerged from his spiritual ordeal he would look like a scarecrow wearing a paper shroud.[1]

The Fighting Parson

In early colonial days there was a striking difference between the people of New England and those of the southern colonies, as to standards of behavior. The Puritan preachers of New England took a firm stand against amusements. Virginians, representing the Church of England, were inclined to let nature take its course. England sometimes sent preachers to the colonies who had not done well back home.

Thus there were many hard-drinking, gambling, cock-fighting parsons, serving churches in the South. One of them got into a fight with his vestrymen and whipped them all. The next Sunday he preached from Nehemiah 13:25:

I contended with them, and cursed them, and smote certain of them, and plucked off their hair.

One Virginia parson fought a duel near his church, and another served as the president of a racing club.[2]

[1] Pitkanen, Allen, "*Jonathan Edwards—Scourger of the Wicked*"; "The Social Studies," October 1946.
[2] Woodward, W. E., *A New American History*, New York, The Literary Guild, 1937.

Turmoil Over Tea; Victory at Sea

The Boston Tea Party

The American Colonists chafed under Britain's onerous taxes. Then the Townshend duties were repealed but for the tax on tea. The effort of England to unload the surplus of tea held by The East India Company, making Americans swallow the hated tax while they bought tea at a bargain price, enraged the colonists in 1773. Led by firebrands like Samuel Adams, they boarded British ships disguised as Indians, broke open hundred of chests, and threw $90,000 worth of tea into the harbor.

Some would snatch up handfuls of tea from the deck and put it in their pockets. Tea, "that painful weed" to some, was a precious commodity to the frugal colonists.

A certain Captain O'Connor came aboard for that purpose and filled his pockets and the lining of his coat with tea. He was ordered to be taken into custody but when he was seized by the skirt of his coat he shed the garment and fled. The crowd on the wharf, aware of the rule-breaker's action, kicked and pummeled him as he ran the gauntlet through the group.[1]

Relations between England and the Colonists went downhill fast after this.

John Paul Jones

This Naval hero of the American Revolution, John Paul Jones, commanded the "Bon Homme Richard" when it fought the British ship, "Serapis" in a duel that lasted for hours. Finally the British Captain demanded that Jones surrender. (They were close enough to hear messages shouted. In fact they were lashed together.) The indomitable American Captain responded, "I have not yet begun to fight." Naval tradition has it that a weary gunner's mate on the second deck, heard the reply, wiped a smoke-stained face and said, "There's always somebody who doesn't get the word." The Navy uses a different word for "somebody."

Finally there was a terrible explosion in the powder magazine of the British ship and soon thereafter the Captain of the "Serapis" surrendered. An American ship, a converted merchantman, had defeated a superior warship.[2]

[1] Commager, Henry Steele, Nevins, Allan, *The Heritage of America*, Boston, Little, Brown and Co., 1939.
[2] Churchill, Winston, *The Age of Revolution*, New York, Dodd, Mead and Company, 1957.

Paul Revere's Ride—On the Water

Paul Revere, dentist, metal-smith, courier, propagandist and officer in the colonial militia, possessed a versatility that reminds one of Thomas Jefferson. It was as a messenger that he gained his fame. Schoolchildren have been told, for centuries, about the signal, "One if by land; two if by sea," from the lanterns in the old church tower which indicated that "The British are coming", the message he was to carry to "every Middlesex village and town."

Before Revere could begin on his famous ride to Lexington, in April 1775, to warn the countryside that the British were coming, he had to get across the Charles River. He needed to avoid troops on land and a British man-of-war guarding the river, cross the water and secure a horse on the other side.

Two friends agreed to row him across, and they met where Revere had his boat hidden. Then he discovered that he had forgotten his spurs and cloth to muffle the oars of the boat. One of his helpers had a girlfriend nearby on North Street. He stood under her window and whistled. There was a quiet conversation, and soon a petticoat was dropped down, still warm. The oars would now be quiet.

Revere wrote a note to his wife, tied it to his dog's collar, and sent him home. Soon he returned with the spurs. Cautiously they rode across the river. Revere leaped to dry land near the old Battery. He secured a horse, and rode to spread the alarm. In a way, he is still riding.

Forbes, Esther, *Paul Revere and the World He Lived In*, Boston, Houghton Mifflin Company, 1942.

Modest Washington

In June, 1775, the Continental Congress took over control of all men under arms. This body had the delicate task of cutting through sectional jealousies, and personal ambitions in order to appoint a commander-in-chief.

Colonel George Washington was the logical choice, with his military experience, aristocratic lineage, and most importantly he represented Virginia, whose support of the American cause was essential. Artemus Ward and John Hancock were also candidates.

Washington aspired for the position but was too modest to say so. He found a way. As a member of Congress he would arrive each day, a towering figure in buff and blue uniform, and take his seat in dignified silence, a patriot sending a quiet message. Washington was appointed, and Hancock publicly demonstrated his disappointment.[1]

Washington's quiet approach carried over to later years. During the meeting of the Constitutional Convention, in Philadelphia, one of the members moved "that the standing army be restricted to 5,000 men at any one time." George Washington, being the chairman, could not offer a motion, but turned to another member and whispered. "Amend the motion to provide that no foreign enemy shall invade the United States at any time with more than 3000 troops."[2]

General Washington's modesty carried over to his military career. He declined pay for his military service but was willing to submit his expense account for repayment. I have seen a copy of one of the forms he sent in, and it was highly detailed, including wine.

[1] Woodward, W. E., *A New American History*, London, Faber and Faber, 1936.

[2] Wilstach, Paul, *Patriots Off Their Pedestals*, (Bobbs/Merrill) as cited by *Reader's Digest*, February, 1950.

Empty Pockets

George Whitefield was one of the powerful preachers of the 18th century. Benjamin Franklin, rationalist though he was, went to hear him preach and fell under the spell of the great orator. At the meeting he perceived that an offering was to be taken at the end of the sermon, and vowed to give nothing. He had, in his pockets, copper, silver, and gold coins. Then he softened, and determined to give the copper. Under the spell of the message, he changed to the silver and then to the gold. The minister finished so admirably that Franklin emptied his pockets into the collection plate.[1]

This is a far cry from Mark Twain, who went to hear a missionary speak. Touched by the description of the plight of those on foreign shores, he decided to put five dollars in the offering. But the speaker droned on and on, and the amount, in his mind, kept dropping, until the sermon ended. After one of his famous pauses, the great humorist admitted, "I stole a nickel out of the plate."

The Mark Twain story is from the oral history of this famous author. In the 1960s I visited an old gentleman, in Jamestown, Tennessee, a ninety-three-year-old lawyer. He told me some interesting stories about Mark Twain and the Clemens family, who used to live there in Fentress County. He also talked about the Scopes trial, in 1925, which he attended. Somewhere I have a booklet he wrote, a history of Fentress County.

Humor connected with taking the collection in Protestant churches, has continued across the years and, has even been put to rhyme:

He put a quarter in the plate,
And meekly raised his eyes.
He had paid another week of rent,
On a mansion in the skies.

There is another story about two tightwads who timed their entry into church after the collection. The preacher noted this and delayed the offering until the men entered the sanctuary. He said to himself, "I've got you this time." But he didn't. One fainted and the other carried him out.

[1] Devens, R. M., *Our First Century*, Springfield, Mass., C. A. Nichols and Company, 1877.

The Battle of Bunker Hill

In June, 1775, General Artemus Ward sent 3,000 Americans to seize and fortify Bunker Hill. By mistake they went to Breed's Hill, and that is where the action occurred and the British attacked. History teachers, across the years, have had to explain that the Battle of Bunker Hill was really fought on Breed's Hill. This is easier than explaining that the Hundred Years War lasted much longer than a century

In the fierce battle the Americans ran short of ammunition. Some were seen chasing British cannon balls as they rolled across the turf, so as to fire them back at the British. A twelve-pound cannon ball would fit any brand of cannon of that caliber.

The British made the mistake of a frontal assault. They had not learned the lesson General Braddock was taught in the French and Indian War. Colonial sharpshooters mowed down the redcoats in great numbers.

Only on the third assault did General Howe and his troops take the American works and that after the Americans ran out of powder. Baldwin says, "The Americans regarded the action as almost a victory."[1]

The French foreign minister observed that with two more such victories the British would have no army left in America. The Ancients would have called this a Pyrrhic victory.

This was a strange and contradictory war. The colonists were declaring loyalty to the King, while claiming they wanted to patch up relations with the mother country. At the same time they were raising armies and shooting down British soldiers. It did not take George III long to describe the situation. Bunker Hill eliminated hopes of reconciliation, and in August, 1775 he proclaimed that the colonies were in rebellion. The colonists fought for fourteen months before taking the bold step of declaring independence.[2]

[1] Baldwin, Leland D. and Kelley, Robert, *The Stream of American History*, Third Edition., New, York, The American Book Company, 1965.
[2] Bailey, Thomas A. and Kennedy, David M., *The American Pageant*, Ninth Edition, Lexington, Mass., D.C. Heath and Company, 1991.

Battle of Cowpens

Whoever heard of an American general, realizing that his untrained troops would run when the battle started, telling them how and when to run? It was January, 1781 when General Daniel Morgan met Lt. Colonel Banastre Tarleton, with a superior British force, in the Battle of Cowpens, in South Carolina.

Morgan selected the field of battle, a level plain with ridges to his rear. His first line was made up of raw militia, recent volunteers, certain to run in the face of the orderly British advance. Morgan made a virtue out of necessity and gave them permission to retire after firing three times. In the second line, 150 yards back, were his seasoned troops, and still further, behind the ridge, his dragoons.

Confidently Tarleton advanced his columns in perfect order, continental style. Morgan rode up and down the lines shouting "three shots, boys, and you are free." When the British were within 100 yards, the Americans fired. Then amazingly they re-loaded and fired twice more. The British were stopped with heavy losses. Then the militiamen pounded around the left and ran for the rear as planned. British cavalry started chasing them only to be met and thrown back by the American dragoons.

Morgan hardly let the men draw a breath before he praised them, urged them to re-load, and marched them around to the right to fire another surprising volley. This, in concert with the action of American dragoons, was the turning point of the battle. Then seasoned American troops swung into action and the British were routed.

Out of a thousand men, Tarleton had 100 killed, including 39 officers, and 229 wounded. Tarleton escaped with a handful of redcoats, but 600 unhurt British soldiers were captured. If one wonders why more than one third of those killed were officers, bear in mind that they were out front, and had white belts criss-crossed on their chests with scarlet coats as a background. They made perfect targets. The Americans had twelve killed and sixty wounded. Cowpens was a notable victory especially after General Gates' defeat by Cornwallis at Camden.[1]

Cowpens has been called "America's most imitated battle." General Morgan demonstrated how militia can be used. This technique was used in three later actions.

[1] Montross, Lynn, "America's Most Imitated Battle," American Heritage, New York, American Heritage Publishing Co., 1950.

Historical Snapshots—18th Century

Bless the British

Tennessee volunteers set out to confront the British during the Revolutionary War. On the night before the Battle of King's Mountain, when they "would come against the British," they called on Bishop Doak to lead in prayer. He prayed for the brave patriots fighting for home and fireside, and then he said, "Now, Lord, bless the British, (At this he had every soldier's interest), whom we expect to see gathered to your bosom, in great numbers."[1]

The World Turned Upside Down

The Revolutionary War reached a climax when General Cornwallis decided to take the war to the South. A French fleet under DeGrasse defeated Graves and his British fleet in the Battle of the Virginia Capes in September, 1781, then Rochambebeau, with a French force of 30,000 and Washington, with 9,000 moved against Cornwallis. Outnumbered, the British general surrendered.

For all practical purposes the war was over.

As 7,021 British troops in brilliant red and white uniforms marched by to stack arms, many wept with shame. To top it all, the band was playing a popular ditty, "The World Turned upside Down." The lines went something like this:

> When I was young and single,
> I went from town to town.
> Then I got married, and,
> The world turned upside down.

The French did far more than send Lafayette to assist America.

The American Revolution had become a world war and the colonists won, only by foreign aid.[2]

King George III

King George III was detested by the American Colonists, except for the loyalists. If you want to see a detailed list of accusations against him, read the Declaration of Independence, with Jefferson filling the role of prosecuting attorney.

It is reported that King George wrote in his diary on July 4, 1776, "Nothing of importance happened today." On this fateful day he lost the American colonies, only to learn about it weeks later.

[1] Reported by A. L. Crabb, Peabody Professor.
[2] Baldwin, Leland D., Kelley, Robert, *The Stream of American History*, New York, The American Book Company, 1965.

Men and Events—Brief Glimpses

Washington on a Roll

After centuries have passed George Washington is remembered as a towering patriotic figure, a symbol of the War for Independence, and the "Father" of our country. His portraits are unsmiling, and why not, for he suffered constant discomfort from ill-fitting false teeth.

However there was another side to this first president. He was a warm, sociable human being who loved to entertain, dance, and play cards. He also had a good sense of humor, and enjoyed a hearty laugh, and an excellent opportunity presented itself.

He went into spasms of laughter, "violent merriment," as one described it, when he came upon two distinguished judges, in the woods near Mount Vernon, without a stitch of clothes on.

John Marshall, (later Chief Justice) and Washington's nephew, Bushrod, had been invited to Mount Vernon for a visit. Since they were traveling together they relied on the services of a single manservant who packed their belongings in a trunk. Somehow the trunk got switched with that of a traveling peddler, at their previous lodging place.

As they approached Mount Vernon the travel-stained men decided to bathe in a small stream and put on fresh clothing. They knew their honored host emphasized good grooming. They stripped, bathed, and then called on the servant to bring fresh clothes. He opened the trunk and found instead, trinkets for sale. There they stood overcome by the naked truth that there was no clean linen.

At this point Washington, out for a walk on his estate, came upon his unclad friends. The ludicrous sight, coupled with the story, meant a Washington, so overcome with laughter, that he rolled on the ground.[1]

Franklin and the Rolls

In 1723 Benjamin Franklin, a seventeen-year-old printer arrived in Philadelphia, tired and dirty from his journey from Boston. He had fallen out with his brother, broken his apprenticeship agreement and was striking out on his own. Franklin later described an event that put him at a disadvantage with the girl who was to become his wife.

Walking up the street he came to a market and saw a boy with bread. Hungry, he found out where the bakery was and went there to buy bread. He asked for biscuit as found in Boston and found they had none. Not realizing the cheap prices, he then asked for three-pennies-worth of any sort of bread. To his surprise, he received three great puffy rolls. He said, "I was surprised at the quantity but took it, and having no room in my pockets, walked off with a roll under each arm, and eating the other."[2]

Soon he passed in front of the Read house, and there was the daughter, later to become his wife, watching, as he described it, his "awkward, ridiculous appearance." He proceeded to the river for a draught of water, and finding himself filled with one roll, gave the other two to a woman and child who had come down the river in a boat with him.

Franklin turned out to be one of the great figures of the Eighteenth Century—printer, inventor, political leader, and diplomat, a favorite in European society.

[1] Storer, Doug, *Stories About the Presidents*, New York, Pocket Books, 1975.
[2] Van Doren, Carl, *Benjamin Franklin*, Garden City, Garden City Publishing Co., 1941.

Amazing Document, The U.S. Constitution

In 1787 an event occurred that changed the course of history—the signing into existence of the United States Constitution. A written constitution was unheard of in the world at that time.

The American Constitution is a unique document, the shortest written constitution in the world, and the oldest such document in existence. It served as a model for other nations to write their constitutions.

It is the foundation of individual freedom. The Bill of Rights was so necessary that a set of amendments was a condition of ratification. The U.S. Constitution represents the fruit of centuries of men's ideas and experience, such as, Magna Carta, actions of the British parliament, the American Colonial experience, indicated by The Mayflower Compact, and Colonial Charters, ideas of lawyers, and philosophers like Locke, Coke, Montesquieu, and Blackstone, and the Declaration of Independence. Churchill said, "The Constitution was a re-affirmation of faith in the principles painfully evolved over the centuries by the English speaking peoples."[1]

The Articles of Confederation (1781–87) was a loose confederation of states, without power to regulate commerce or to levy taxes, and with no federal courts. How would you like to carry on a government financed by voluntary contributions?

The needs of the new nation were not being met and a convention was called in Philadelphia, in 1787, *for the sole and express purpose of revising the Articles of Confederation*. A total of 55 delegates from 12 states assembled at the brick state-house in Philadelphia on May 25, 1787. Rhode Island sent no delegates. The men who gathered were of high caliber, "demi-gods," as Jefferson called them.

Among the giants were Washington, elected chairman, Benjamin Franklin, the elder statesman; James Madison, who made so many significant contributions that he is called "The Father of the Constitution"; and Alexander Hamilton, who wanted a stronger federal government but helped "sell" this one by his essays in *The Federalist*.

Absent were the ardent revolutionary leaders: Jefferson, Paine, Samuel Adams, Hancock, and Patrick Henry who suspected a centralizing move and refused to attend.

Within five days a bold step was taken when the delegates decided to scrap the Articles of Confederation, despite explicit instructions from Congress to revise. In effect they agreed to overthrow the existing government by peaceful means. They then moved to form a new government.

Heated issues divided the group and there was imminent danger that the meeting would break up in failure. A need for divine guidance was evident, and skeptical, old Benjamin Franklin proposed that the daily sessions be opened with prayer. At this point the dissension lessened. In the face of divisive issues, the American genius for compromise emerged.

Throughout the sticky, steamy summer of 1789, the delegates worked in secrecy, guards posted at the door. The Constitution that resulted was "a bundle of compromises," and this spirit continued throughout the ratification process, encouraged by a promise of a Bill of Rights. It was finally signed by thirty-nine delegates on September 17, 1787, to become effective when nine of the thirteen states ratified it.

Franklin, who opposed portions of the Constitution, urged its adoption, saying it was the best they were likely to get. While the last members were signing, Franklin pointed out to nearby delegates, the picture of a rising sun painted on the back of the speaker's chair. He mentioned that in the midst of struggle, hopes, and fears that "often and often" he had wondered if it were a rising or setting sun. He then said, "I have the happiness to know, it is a rising, and not a setting sun."[2]

The Constitution provides a government by the people, a limited government, checks and balances, a federal government (shared powers), a separation of powers, and the supremacy of national, over state governments. It was the other way round with the Articles of Confederation.

The Constitution provided for a republic (which it still is in legal structure) but gave it the flexibility to become a democracy. It did this by the Bill of Rights and other amendments, by Court decisions, and by customs and usages.

The story is told of a lady who asked Franklin, after the Convention was over, "Well, Doctor, what have we got, a republic or a monarchy?" He answered, "A republic if you can keep it."[3]

[1] Churchill, Winston, *The Age of Revolution*, New York, Dodd, Mead and Company, 1957.
[2] Commager, Henry Steele, *Living Ideas in America,* New York, Harper and Brothers, 1951.
[3] Bailey, Thomas R., Kennedy, David M., *The American Pageant*, Ninth edition, Lexington, Mass., D. C. Heath and Company, 1961.

III

The Nineteenth Century

A Pocketful of Rice

Thomas Jefferson, like Washington, was much interested in farm products and scientific improvement of crops. Rice, one of the three main crops in the South, had his special interest.

A delicious and highly nutritive wild rice grew in the Pontine Marshes in Italy. It was so desirable that the authorities slapped a complete embargo on its exportation. Thomas Jefferson, Minister to France, visited the Italian marsh region, and was enthralled by the rice. As he meandered along, he plucked off the grains and stored them in his capacious coat pocket. This successful smuggler planted the prized grains in the Carolina marsh region where this wild rice still grows.[1]

Jefferson exulted over the feat with a farmer friend in the Carolinas. However, a search of his correspondence with John Adams, during this period, reveals no mention of his escapade. I think he respected that strict New England conscience and wanted to avoid a scolding.

Jefferson believed in a strict interpretation of the Constitution which would deny the President's right to purchase territory without the consent of Congress. But the opportunity was fleeting, so he bought half a continent at a bargain price.

The "strict interpretation" is still a heated issue and many judges, departing from it, have been inclined to legislate from the bench.

[1] Cerf, Bennett, *Try and Stop Me*, New York, Simon and Schuster, 1044, quoting Neal McNeill of the *New York Times*.

Bathwater and the Louisiana Purchase

For several months in the spring of 1803, Robert S. Livingston, U. S. Ambassador to France, had pestered Napoleon with proposals to buy New Orleans for the U. S., to no avail. Then, the First Consul decided that Louisiana would be lost to England anyway and shocked Livingston by offering to sell all the vast territory. James Monroe joined Livingston to consummate the deal. From this purchase all, or parts, of 13 states would be carved.

Upon hearing of the proposed sale, Napoleon's two brothers, Lucien, who had made the treaty securing the territory, and Joseph, who had been given the throne of Naples, tried to dissuade him from a step that would arouse the indignation of the nation.

Lucien and Joseph went to the Tuileries palace and found Napoleon in his bath, the water opaque with perfume. They protested the sale and said the Chambers would never give consent. Napoleon declared he would do it without the consent of parliament or anyone else. Then Joseph threatened to lead the opposition. He said if Napoleon persisted, they would all probably join the other victims of Napoleonic justice. Out-reasoned and outraged, Napoleon rose up and threw himself back into the bathwater, drenching both of them. With quick wit Lucien began quoting, in a theatrical tone, Neptune, rebuking the waves, according to Virgil. At this the three brothers recovered their good humor. The valet, standing by, fainted and fell to the floor. The dispute ended and the United States got a real estate bargain.[1]

President Thomas Jefferson, a strict constructionist, doubted that he had the right to make the purchase. However he knew the opportunity was about to pass, and he seized it. He later said, "I did a little wrong to do a great right." The sale price was fifteen million dollars.

[1] Adams, Henry, *History of the United States*, V. II, New York, Charles Scribner's Sons, 1903.

Jackson Refuses to Retreat

The War of 1812 was fought mainly with volunteers. At a time of crisis in 1814, prior to the battle of Horseshoe Bend, Andrew Jackson received advice from Governor Blount to retreat. This was because enlistments from volunteers had expired. With troops facing starvation, General Andrew Jackson wrote an indomitable letter (while racked with pain from a shattered shoulder, and dysentery) to Governor Blount:

Arouse from your lethargy—despite fawning smiles or snarling frowns—with energy, exercise your function—the campaign must rapidly progress or your country ruin. Call out the full quota—arrest the officer who omits his duty, and let popularity perish for the moment. Save Mobile, save the territory—save your frontier from being drenched in blood. What, retrograde under these circumstances? I will perish first.

Your obedient servant,
Andrew Jackson, Major General, Tennessee Militia[1]

A few months later Jackson headed for New Orleans where he defeated General Pakenham and a superior British army. He sent scouts ahead to blaze a trail and they did this by cutting three notches in trees along the way. One of the trees was a huge oak in my Grandfather Tipton's front yard in the Straughn Community, south of Rose Hill, Alabama. This "Three Notch Oak" blew down in a storm in 1926. Judging from the size of the stump, I considered it a huge tree. The road in front of our farm went into Andalusia, the county seat, where it is named "Three Notch Street." General Jackson, you left your mark in south Alabama.

[1] Grant, H. W., *Andrew Jackson*, New York, Doubleday, 2005.

Madison Flees Washington

The reality of military conflict came home to Americans during the War of 1812. In August of 1814 an attack on Washington, D.C. by a British force of about 4,500 men, seemed imminent. The American position was precarious for the Capital was defended only by raw militia troops. Madison's Secretary of War, John Armstrong, seemed curiously uninterested in planning a defense of the city. He was chafing, perhaps from a recent rebuke by the President, for appointing Andrew Jackson as a Major-General without Madison's approval.

The military commander, General Winder, made a serious blunder when he withdrew the militia from the Bladensburg Road, the most likely route for the British advance. He fell back to the city where many of his militia went home for the night.

Somebody needed to do something so the next day Madison took to the field himself. He hoped to get Armstrong to work out some sort of defense with General Winder. He narrowly missed blundering into enemy troops before he met with Armstrong and Winder. The unenergetic Secretary of War had given no orders, and the President remarked that there was still time to do so. At this point Armstrong rode up to Winder and said a few words to him. The President wanted to join the two, but at that moment his horse became unruly and he never learned what was said.

Then the battle began and the Americans made a poor showing. The militia broke and ran almost as soon as the firing began. Seeing that the battle was lost, Madison and some of his cabinet members retired to the city. He rode amid a stream of citizens, fleeing soldiers, and cabinet members.

Meantime Joshua Barney, having sunk his gunboats, took 400 sailors and defended the road at the district line. He and his men maintained an energetic resistance to the entire British force for nearly two hours. His heroic action so impressed the British that they treated him with courtesy out of proportion to his rank when he was captured. His strong defense permitted the frightened militia to make their escape.

When the President arrived at the White House, he found that his wife, Dolley, had already departed with several wagon loads of baggage. His dinner was ready and on the table but he did not linger to enjoy it. He escaped to the Virginia woods. British officers ate the meal and then set fire to the White House. I think the British have always been a bit ashamed of this action. One could conclude that Andrew Jackson evened the score the next year at the Battle of New Orleans.

Smith, Albert Emerson, *James Madison: Builder*, New York, Wilson-Erickson, 1937.

Dirty Politics—1824

The disputed presidential election of 1824 was marked by rancor and political bargaining. With no clear-cut decision by the Electoral College the matter was referred to the House of Representatives. Jackson, J. Q. Adams and Crawford were candidates. Clay was eliminated but worked behind the scene for Adams, who was favorable to Clay's "American System." Adams was elected, New York being the swing state, and by one vote in that state. When the Secretary of State appointment was offered to Clay, cries of "corrupt bargain" arose from the Jackson camp.

Senator John Randolph acidly commented that the union of Adams and Clay was a coalition of "a puritan and a blackleg". In a senate speech he asked, "Who is this being so brilliant and so corrupt, who, like a rotten mackerel in the moonlight, shines and stinks?"[1] Clay called him out and they fought a duel. Both missed.

When the presidential election of 1824 was thrown into the House of Representatives, it became clear that the New York delegation would decide the matter. These representatives were so divided that it became apparent that Rep. Stephen Van Rensselaer's vote was crucial. He wavered between Crawford and Adams but decided on the former. Just before the voting box reached him he leaned forward, put his head down, and prayed to his Maker for guidance. Then his eyes opened, and there on the floor below him was a ticket bearing the name of John Quincy Adams. He took it as a sign from heaven, picked up the ticket, put it in the voting box, and cast the deciding vote for Adams.[2]

It is interesting to note that in the disputed election of 2,000, there was a serious possibility that the election would be decided by the House of Representatives. As it turned out, the Supreme Court decided the issue; Bush, with fewer popular votes than Gore, was elected.

[1] Adams, Henry, *John Randolph*, Boston, Houghton Miflin and Co., 1894.
[2] Van Buren, Martin, *The Autobiography of Martin Van Buren*, U.S. Government Printing Office, Washington, D.C., 1920.

Historic Glimpses in the 1800s

Audubon and the Climbing Rattlesnake

Frontiersmen were tellers of tall tales and much of their exaggeration had to do with the richness of their soil. Thus one pioneer boasted that he planted spikes at night and harvested crowbars the next day. Scientists were not immune from the tendency to stretch the truth. John J. Audubon told of seeing a rattlesnake leaping from limb to limb in a treetop, in pursuit of a squirrel. Some snakes climb trees but not rattlesnakes.

In discussing wildlife in America with British scientists he was judged imaginative and undependable. One Briton said, of the rattlesnake story, "this is really too much for us Englishmen to swallow, whose gullets are known to be the largest, the widest and the most elastic in the world."[1]

Lafayette and the Shipload of Gifts

The young Marquis de Lafayette received honors and acclaim while fighting for American independence. America's regard for him increased with the years. At the age of 67 he revisited the country for which he had shed his blood. He was the guest of the nation, when in 1824, he visited the United States. The year-long visit was one great triumphal tour. While in Washington he was presented with a gift of $200,000.

Gifts from states, cities, and organizations poured in and he became worried about how he could get them home to France. The government solved the problem by putting at his disposal a ship, the frigate *Brandywine*, bearing the name of his first battle. He and his son, George Washington Lafayette, and the shipload of gifts, returned, in style, to France.[2]

[1] Clark, Thomas D., *The Rampaging Frontier*, Indianapolis, The Bobbs-Merrill Co., 1939.
[2] Loth, David, *The People's General, The Personal Story of Lafayette*, New York, Charles Scribner's Sons, 1951.

Yankee Inventiveness

The 1800s was an era of inventions in America and this started long before the Civil War. The machines of New England poured forth a stream of tools, wire, nails, bolts, and screws. More importantly the universal milling machine, turret lathe, and the grinding machine, made possible an amazing precision and economy of production.

Brass Clocks

In the early 1830s wooden clocks cost five dollars and metal clocks ten times that much. That quickly changed. In 1838 Chauncey Jerome began using the plan of interchangeable parts to manufacture brass clocks that sold for fifty cents. A shipment to England of these cheap clocks at an invoice price of $1.50, caught the attention of British customs officials. They thought he was trying to cheat them on the duty cost, and, to teach him a lesson, bought the whole shipment at $1.50 each. Jerome was delighted and sent another shipment, which was seized and payment made. Only when the third shipment arrived, did the British realize that the Yankee clockmaker had gotten the best of them.[1]

Eli Whitney

Eli Whitney, a Yankee from Connecticut, while living in Georgia, invented the cotton gin (engine) in 1793. It enabled a worker to separate from the seeds of short-staple cotton, twenty times as much cotton, as picking it by hand. The machine was so simple that he could not get a patent for it. However, it was revolutionary in its result, turning the South into the "cotton kingdom," and encouraging the growth of slavery.

Whitney returned to Connecticut and devoted his energies to gun manufacture. Using the newly invented machine tools, he worked out the principle of interchangeable parts in his gun factory, and modern manufacturing methods resulted. No longer would a gunsmith toil for days to produce one musket. He secured a contract with Jefferson's administration for 10,000 muskets and produced them with remarkable speed.

In the 1850s a clerk in the U. S. Patent Office resigned because he saw no future. He figured that everything that could be invented had been invented.

[1] Baldwin, Leland D., and Kelley, Robert, *The Stream of American History*, (third edition), New York, American Book Company, 1965.

Indians, Webster, and Marshall

In the first two decades of the 19th Century a series of Supreme Court decisions, handed down by John Marshall, greatly strengthened the Federal Government. In the Dartmouth College Case the Court ruled against the act of the New Hampshire legislature to alter the ancient charter of the College. The Court was influenced by the eloquent plea made by Daniel Webster on behalf of the College, his alma mater. He said, "She is a small college but there are those who love her."

While working on the case he told the college president that the charter made clear that it was founded for the purpose of civilizing and instructing Indians. Yet no Indians had been enrolled for a long time and this might endanger the case. He thought it would be well, if the president would go into Canada and bring some of the Aborigines into the walls of the College. He did so and found three choice specimens. They got in the boat and headed across the river. They were struck with wonder about the buildings on the bank, which looked more and more like a prison. The Indian at the bow of the boat gave a significant look at the others, and uttered a war whoop. Over the side they went and swam to the north shore. The astonished president called and entreated them to come back, to no avail. They disappeared into the woods.[1] President Wheelock's student recruitment plan failed. Daniel Webster had to pursue the case without Indians.

John Marshall's Court

The case of Dartmouth College vs. Woodward (1819) was only one of several Supreme Court decisions that contributed to judicial nationalism. John Marshall assumed the top judicial position in 1801, and during his three decades of tenure transformed the weakest branch of government into the strongest. Bailey called Marshall the "Molding Father" of the Constitution, and Daniel Webster, who often appeared before the Court, the "Expounding Father."[2]

Marshall interpreted the Constitution along centralizing lines in the spirit of Hamilton's federalism. But he came up against a strong adversary in President Andrew Jackson. The issue was the re-chartering of the Bank of The United States in 1832. Jackson vetoed the bill on the grounds that the Bank was unconstitutional. Marshall had already ruled the Bank constitutional in McCulloch vs. Maryland. Now Jackson seemed to be declaring the Executive Branch of government more powerful than Congress or the Supreme Court. Marshall ruled against Jackson and the President responded with the same attitude he had in the Worcester vs. Georgia case when he said, "John Marshall has made his decision; now let him enforce it." He withdrew federal funds from the Bank and put them in state banks.

[1] Harvey, Peter, *Reminiscences and Anecdotes of Daniel Webster*, Boston, Little, Brown and Co. 1877.
[2] Bailey, Thomas A. and Kennedy, David M., *The American Pageant*, ninth edition, Lexington, Mass., D. C. Heath and Company, 1987.

Friends of the Common Man

Davy Crockett and His Campaign Tactics

Davy Crockett, the noted bear-hunter and Indian fighter from Tennessee, made no pretense of being an orator or of knowing anything about politics. Yet he was elected to the Tennessee Legislature, and later, to the United States Congress. His shrewd wit and boundless good humor earned him many friends before his untimely death at the Alamo in 1836.

While running for the Legislature in 1821 he attended a combination barbecue, squirrel hunt, and political gathering. He and his opponent were expected to make speeches. He arose and told the audience they "knowed" what he came for—their votes, and if they weren't careful he would get them. The crowd laughed heartily. Then he tried to make a speech but choked up. He confessed that he was like the man beating on a barrel that once had cider in it, who explained he was trying to get some out. Crockett commented that, like that man, he had a speech in him but just couldn't get it out. The crowd roared. Then he told them a few anecdotes. After a few minutes he remarked that his throat was as dry as a powder-horn and suggested a trip to the liquor stand. Most of the crowd followed him. He continued with jests and jokes while his opponent with "mighty few left to hear him" finished his oration. Crockett won the election.[1]

The Scramble for Jackson's Cheese

Representing the new states of the West, Andrew Jackson brought with him to the White House the frontier philosophy that vigor and self-reliance, rather than birth and wealth, were the marks of distinction. Jacksonian democracy was vividly illustrated, near the end of his second term, when he invited the public to share with him a large gift of cheese.

A devoted follower of Jackson, Colonel Meecham of New York, decided to show his regard with pounds of cheese. He intended it to surpass, in size and quality, the one sent by the farmers of Massachusetts to President Jefferson. Thus a huge cheese, weighing fourteen hundred pounds (Jefferson's weighed only seven hundred and fifty) arrived decked with roses at the White House in 1836. It was put away to ripen. The next year the President announced that the cheese would be cut on February 22, 1837. The public was invited to come to the White House to sample the cheese.

Early in the morning the public started its march to the White House. They came in vehicles of all sorts, some from as far away as Alexandria and Baltimore. The Senate, caught up in the excitement, adjourned; the House did not.

Pandemonium reigned at the White House as the surging throngs tore into the cheese with knives, spoons, and fingers. People fought their way through the crowd carrying redolent hunks of cheese. Fragments were trodden underfoot and carpets and furniture were sticky with it. The President mingled with the throng and enjoyed watching the scramble for the cheese.

President-elect Van Buren was present at the "cheese excitement" and vowed that nothing like this would happen in his regime.[2]

[1] Commager, Henry Steele, and Nevins, Allen, *The Heritage of America*, Boston, Little, Brown and Co., 1939.
[2] Colman, Edna M., *Seventy-five Years of White House Gossip*, New York, Doubleday, 1925.

Warfare in Jackson's Cabinet

An episode in President Andrew Jackson's first term seemed like a minor problem but it led to a Cabinet upheaval. The dispute, which raged around Peggy O'Neil Eaton, was aptly termed by Van Buren, "The Eaton Malaria."

Peggy O'Neill was the vivacious, though somewhat unconventional, daughter of an Irish tavern keeper. Jackson had stopped at the tavern and had become acquainted with Peggy and her father. She had married a navy man who had been declared dead after he was missing at sea, before she met and married Senator John Eaton. When Eaton joined Jackson's cabinet a tempest arose. The other cabinet wives, led by Mrs. Calhoun, looked askance at the lively Peggy and snubbed her at social occasions. At one reception she was stranded with only the President and Van Buren paying attention to her. Van Buren, a bachelor, had no wife to answer to when he got home.

President Jackson was furious. Motivated by his regard for the common man (and woman) and with the memory of mistreatment his own wife had suffered, Jackson swung into action, laying down the law to his cabinet members.

Things came to a head when the cabinet wives boycotted an official dinner because Mrs. Eaton was to be present. Jackson knew no middle ground. He gave his cabinet members, caught between a rock and a hard place, an ultimatum. The Eatons were there to stay and if they could not accept this they should resign.

Van Buren, with dreams of the presidency, resigned so that the others would. A new cabinet was appointed. Who would have thought that social snobbery would overturn a Cabinet?

The story had a pleasant ending for the vivacious Peggy. Eaton was named Minister to Spain and Peggy was received with open arms in the highest social circles and became a good friend of the Queen.

There was a political fall-out, as the acrimony between Jackson and Calhoun increased.

Passett, John Spencer, *The Life of Andrew Jackson*, New York, The Macmillan Co., 1931.
Lecture by Dr. Fremont Wirth, graduate school, George Peabody College.

Struggles of Hugh Glass

The dangers of the frontier west, the ferocity of grizzly bears, and a glimpse of man's indomitable spirit, all come together in the story of Hugh Glass. He was one of many trappers and explorers who went west after the Lewis and Clark expedition opened up that vast area. Hugh Glass was a member of Andrew Henry's party, which started for the Yellowstone Valley in the fall of 1823.

He was a hunter, and, out ahead of the party, he was confronted by a grizzly bear and her cubs. Before he could retreat or shoot, she seized him, and bit out a chunk of flesh for her cubs. The she began mauling him. He screamed for help but before his fellows could arrive and kill the bear he had been mangled from head to foot.

Henry and the others were convinced Glass would soon die, and paying two of the men to stay with him, the party moved on. He lingered, and five days later his volunteer nurses abandoned him, taking his gun, knife, flint and other essentials with them. They reported to Henry that Glass had died.

When Glass awoke and realized what had happened, he was filled with rage. This gave him reason for living. He lay around, eating wild fruit and berries, and then started to drag himself to Fort Kiowa, 100 miles away. He came upon wolves attacking a buffalo calf. Waiting until they had killed it, he chased them away, and ate the flesh raw. Then he took some with him to sustain him on the painful trip.

He finally arrived at the fort where he met another party of trappers leaving for the Yellowstone. In spite of his condition he joined them and headed west again. The trappers were attacked by Indians and all were killed but Glass. He survived and arrived at Fort Tilton where he secured a kit and started on the trail of those who had deserted him.

All alone on the trail, he had only his flint and knife. Young buffalo calves were everywhere and he was able to get plenty of food. He said, "These little fixin's make a man feel right pert when he is three or four hundred miles away from anybody or anywhere."[1]

He finally arrived at the fort and confronted those who had deserted him. But the nine month journey had diminished his rage. Nothing happened.

Glass was preceded by John Colter who left the Lewis and Clark expedition in 1806 to go to the Yellowstone area. DeVoto called him the "first mountain man."[2] Many credit him with the discovery of the land of the thousand smokes. The story of his spectacular escape from the Blackfeet Indians is a saga of its own.

[1] Federal Writers Project of the Works Progress Administration, *The Oregon Trail* (American Guide Series), New York, Hastings House, 1939.
[2] DeVoto, Bernard, *Across the Wide Missouri*, Boston, Houghton Mifflin Company, 1947.

The Pathmaker in Action

When the United States went to war with Mexico in 1846, the vast territory of California was already in possession of Americans. John C. Fremont, the explorer, was the leader in the "Bear Flag" war that wrested California from Mexico and declared it a republic. When the news came of the battles on the Rio Grande, the stars and stripes replaced the bear flag. The California republic did not last as long as that of Texas. Lt. Colonel Fremont was appointed Governor by Commodore Stockton, the naval Commander.

This did not set well with General Kearney who thought his orders meant that he was Governor and that he was Commander in Chief, not Stockton. The dispute finally ended in a court-martial resulting in Fremont's resignation under pressure. In the midst of this wrangle, Fremont made a theatrical ride from Los Angeles to Monterey to warn Kearney of a rumored Mexican uprising.

Accompanied by Don Jesus Pico and his black servant, he left at daybreak on a round trip of eight hundred and forty miles in eight days. Each man had three horses, and the six loose mounts were driven before them. They changed horses every twenty miles. At a fast gallop they traveled a hundred and twenty miles on the first day, March 22, 1847. They slept that night at a ranch near Santa Barbara and the next night, after covering one hundred and thirty-five miles, at San Luis Obispo. Here they made a complete change of horses. They rode seventy miles the next day and slept in a canyon where their sleep was interrupted by prowling bears. The next day they rode ninety miles, arriving at mid-afternoon at Kearney's headquarters in Monterey.

After a day in conference with the domineering Kearney, they made a rapid trip back to Los Angeles. Fremont had covered, in seventy-six riding hours, a distance equal to that from Chicago to New York. The word of this exploit made news in the West for years to come.

Fremont went on to run for President on the Republican ticket in 1856. Their banner was "Free Soil, Free Speech, and Fremont." He carried eleven states but lost to Buchanan.

He returned to the Army in the Civil War and was put in command of the Department of the West. In Missouri he took the rash action of confiscating property of the Secessionists and freeing their slaves. He got into President Lincoln's political sphere and was relieved of his command. Like Custer and the MacArthurs he had a hard time remembering who was boss.

Nevins, Allan, *Fremont, Pathmaker of the West*, New York, Appleton-Century Co., 1939.
Baldwin, Leland D. and Kelley, Robert, *The Stream of American History*, Third Edition, New York, American Book Company, 1965.

Food on the Frontier

Food was a constant concern on the Great Plains, in the Rockies, and in California after the gold rush began. Buffalo meat was the staple on the plains and in the mountains. When trappers were hired by a fur-trading company, the contract would often contain the promise of eight pounds of buffalo meat a day. A trapper would consume three pounds of steak or tongue for supper and then broil ribs over the dying embers before turning in. This meat is described as the most nutritious of all foods, and the Cheyenne and Blackfeet Indians subsisted entirely on it, in good health.

One group of travelers fell in with friendly Indians who offered them meat. Inquiring by signs as to what kind, they were assured by seeing fingers held above the head that it was deer meat. They ate heartily, but on leaving the camp, they spied hide and long ears indicating that a mule had been slaughtered. It was not venison, but a favorite food of the Indians, mule meat, that they had eaten.

John C. Fremont, in an exploration, about 1840, in what became Utah, was fascinated by great numbers of insect larvae which washed up on the shore of The Great Salt Lake. An old hunter, Joseph Walker, told him of a party of explorers who came upon a group of Indian families camped on the shore of a salt lake. The Indians fled, leaving behind in their lodges, bags of what appeared to be fish, dried and pounded.

The starving trappers ate a hearty supper and were planning an abundant breakfast, when it was discovered that they had eaten worms from the salt lake. The stomachs of the trappers couldn't tolerate the idea of this repulsive food and quickly ejected it.[1] It might have helped if they had known that grubs and larvae are consumed around the world as nutritious food.

The Gold Rush started in 1848 and those surviving the overland trip suffered incredible hardships. When they arrived in Sacramento the problem of shelter and food awaited them. The women seemed most distressed by the food—rancid pork that was shipped from New York, around the Horn, butter that had turned brown, and flour, filled with weevils and worms. Cows abounded in California but there were no dairy products for sale. There was some dried fruit from Chile, yams and onions, from the Sandwich Islands, and seagull eggs from the Farallones, selling for a dollar each.

The people were starved for flavors, sweet, sour and salt. One man, with such a longing, bought for himself molasses and vinegar. Sitting on a log, he mixed the two and sopped them with bread, oblivious to the crowd around him.[2] Little did he know that, a century and a half later, these would be touted as health foods.

[1] Nevins, Allan, Fremont, *Pathmarker of the West*, New York, Appleton-Century Co, 1939.
[2] Paden, Irene D., *The Wake of the Prairie Schooner*, New York, The Macmillan Co., 1943.

The Pony Express

In the 1850s the populous Eastern half of the nation was separated from the growing west coast by vast stretches of plains and mountains. Railroads were not yet built across the continent. How to communicate? Letters took months to travel from California to New York around Cape Horn.

Then came the Pony Express. The idea of a fast mail service, by rider, between Missouri and California was the dream of William M. Guin.

The Pony Express contracted to carry the mail over the 1,966 mile route in ten days. Each rider traveled from 75 to 125 miles. The first run started from Sacramento, California on April 3, 1860 and on the same day, from St. Joseph, Missouri.

A hundred stations were built in wild country and had to be maintained. Riders, totaling eighty, were recruited and trained. Heavyweights were not sought; rather medium-sized, muscular men, at home in the saddle were hired. Riding at top speed, these wiry men would leap from one horse, mount another, saddled and waiting, and ride like the wind. Defense against Indians and outlaws? Outrun them!

Starting at St. Joseph, Missouri the route led through Fort Kearney, Nebraska; Fort Laramie, Wyoming; Fort Bridger, Wyoming; Great Salt Lake, and Camp Floyd, Utah; Carson City, Nevada; Wasatch Silver Mines, Nevada; Placerville, California; and finally Sacramento, California.

Perhaps the most famous of the riders were William (Buffalo Bill) Cody and Wild Bill Hickock. It was an uncurried crew. Buffalo Bill went on to serve as hunter for a transcontinental railroad construction crew. He provided wild turkeys as well as buffalo meat to the ravenous workers.

Then progress caught up with this adventurous enterprise. The telegraph line between Omaha and San

Francisco was completed in October, 1861 and the Pony Express went out of business. Its one year of service, with all the romance, color and example of excellent organization, has caused Americans to remember the Pony Express as a vivid chapter in the nation's history.

Various secondary sources.

Cartwright and the Mud-Hole Sermon

The style and activities of itinerant frontier preachers are astonishing. One of the best-known of these was the dauntless and muscular Peter Cartwright. Community bullies who thought it fun to duck the preacher in the creek were reluctant to try it with him. He also knew how to respond to other kinds of persecution.

Cartwright was preaching in Southern Illinois and his "fire and brimstone" sermons stirred up opposition. Riding along a country road he overtook two young men and a girl in a two-horse wagon. They began to taunt him, imitating his mourners. The incensed preacher tried to get away from his tormenters but his horse was lame and they stayed close.

They approached a long mud-hole. The preacher took to the bridle path and began to draw away. The driver whipped the horses and entered the mud-hole at full speed. He did not see a large stump on the right side. The fore wheel rode up on the stump and overturned the wagon. The young men gave a wild leap and wound up in the mud and water, waist deep. The young lady, dressed in white, sprang as far as she could and landed on all fours, her hands sunk in the mud and her face in the water. She would have drowned but her friends pulled her up and out. The preacher turned his horse and rode back to watch the ludicrous situation. He rose up in his stirrups and began to shout "Glory to God! Hallelujah! Another sinner's down! Glory to God! Hallelujah! Glory! Hallelujah!"[1]

He was convinced that they hated preachers, especially Methodist preachers, so he preached to them, warning them that this should be the last time they insulted a preacher. He wound up by saying, "The next time God will serve you worse and the devil will get you."[2]

[1] Hart, A. B., *American History Told By Contemporaries*, New York, The McMillan Co., 1937–38.
[2] Ibid.

Rough and Ready Taylor

Zachary Taylor had a brilliant record in the Mexican War and this elected him President of the United States in 1848. He was "ready" to confront the enemy. Under heavy fire he was urged to withdraw. His response was to move closer to the enemy so the shots would pass overhead.

The "rough" part of his nickname was illustrated by casual attire, including a floppy palmetto hat. Word of this got around and at a meeting with Flag Officer Conner of the Navy, it posed a dilemma. Knowing that naval officers "wore all the uniform the law allows," Taylor dug a brigadier general's uniform out of a trunk and dressed up. Meantime Conner, to put Taylor at ease, discarded his uniform and appeared in civilian clothes. Embarrassment was mutual. Their respective staffs broke up in laughter.[1]

Though not seeking it Zachary Taylor was nominated by the Whigs in 1848 as their candidate for President. Old "Rough and Ready" was not ready. He was not at the convention and was notified by mail. The letter informing him of his nomination arrived with postage due and he did not pick it up. He did not know for several months that he was his party's nominee. He did run and was elected.[2]

His reluctance to run is exceeded only by W.T. Sherman whose classic statement is still quoted: "I will not run if nominated and will not serve if elected."

[1] Lewis, Lloyd, *Captain Sam Grant*, Boston, Little, Brown and Company, 1950.
[2] Announced by Walter Conkrite during the 1976 Democratic Convention.

Revivalism in America in the 1800s

The Nineteenth Century was marked by outstanding religious revivals, carrying on the "Great Awakening" tradition of the previous century. There was the great spiritual event in 1801 at Cane Ridge, Kentucky, called by some, "the mother of all revivals." It was planned by Presbyterian preachers as a camp meeting to create some enthusiasm in a spiritually dormant frontier religious world. It succeeded beyond their wildest dreams.

During the week of August 6–13, 1801, a huge crowd, estimated at 10,000 to 25,000 gathered in a rural area where there was a log cabin church, near Lexington, Kentucky. Here there was singing, praying, and preaching, by as many as five ministers preaching at once, in different parts of the campground. Denominational barriers disappeared. This "American Pentecost" was accompanied by some ecstatic behavior-groaning, shouting, holy laughter, and being "slain in the spirit" (falling into a coma).

Though some were involved in religious hysteria, the crowds participated in a deeply spiritual event where sin was confronted and people were exhorted to lead holy lives. Out of the Cane Ridge meeting came some significant results—the creation of at least two new denominations, The Christian Church (Disciples of Christ), and the Cumberland Presbyterian Church as well as the camp meeting movement, led mainly by the Methodists during the rest of the century. The great "American Pentecost" at Cane Ridge revitalized religion on the frontier, raised a higher moral standard, and led to the emergence of outstanding Protestant evangelists later in the century.

Conklin considered the Cane Ridge experience "the most important religious gathering in all of American history, both for what it symbolized and from the effects that flowed from it."[1]

Charles G. Finney was one of the most powerful preachers of the Gospel to appear on the American scene. Sometimes whole towns were converted; courts were adjourned, theaters were deserted, and a veritable reign of terror seemed to seize the ungodly during his meetings. Trained for a legal profession, he added a lawyer's logic to the talents of a frontier preacher.

In one meeting he interceded in his prayer so forcefully that people fell into the aisles and screamed for mercy. He had to intervene and assure them that they were not in hell yet and pled with them to turn to Christ.

Finney could hold an audience spellbound for an hour or more, playing on their emotions in a strong voice that ranged from pathos to condemnation. As he would preach to one section of the crowd and then whirl to point at another group, they would duck as though to avoid punishment. He would describe a sinner's descent into hell by pointing his finger at the ceiling and slowly bringing it down, as he traced the downward path of the soul to perdition. People in the back of the crowd would involuntarily come to their feet to see what was happening.[2]

Peter Cartwright was a powerful preacher of the mid-century as well. In the last part of the century and in the early 1900s, A. M. Hills, a disciple of Finney, his president at Oberlin College, carried on the practice of eloquent revival preaching. He was in the Wesleyan holiness tradition, broader than his Congregationalist background. Hills' preached, wrote thirty-five books, 3,000 articles, and was founding president of three colleges.[3] Dwight L. Moody was probably the best known evangelist in the late 1800s.

The great revivals of the 1800s had significant social results. Just as the Wesleyan revival in England, in the 1700s, helped weaken the slave trade and focus on abuses in English society, revivalism in America had beneficial social outcomes as well. John Wesley had fought slavery and encouraged Wilberforce to "Stay the course." This political leader campaigned so effectively that the British slave trade was declared illegal in 1807 and abolished in the British Empire in 1833.

In America, revivalists like Finney attacked the institution of slavery and vigorously supported prison reform. Timothy Smith skillfully connected revivals and beneficial social results in his significant book, *Revivalism and Social Reform*.[4]

[1] Conkin, Paul K., *Cane Ridge; America's Pentecost*, Madison, Wisconsin, University of Wisconsin Press, 1990.

[2] Thomas, Benjamin F., *Theodore Weld*, New Brunswick, N. J., Rutgers University Press, 1950.
[3] Gresham, L. Paul, *Waves Against Gibralter*, A Memoir of Dr. A. M. Hills, Bethany, OK, Southern Nazarene University Press, 1992.
[4] Smith, Timothy, *Revivalism and Social Reform*, New York, Aberdeen Press, 1957.

Quarrelsome Congressmen

Senator Fracas

In the mid-1800s there was much ill feeling in the Senate over Clay's effort at compromise, the Omnibus Bill. A disgraceful altercation broke out on the Senate floor between Senators Benton and Foote. They had already exchanged heated words over the admission of California. Foote was defending a motion to submit the plans of Clay, Bell, Douglas, and others to a select committee of thirteen.

Benton broke in to charge that this was an attempt to throw it into a flame, and that the country had been terrified by the cry of "Wolf, wolf." Foote stoutly defended his friends, victims of calumniators. At the use of this word, Benton left his desk and strode toward Foote. The Mississippian retreated toward the clerk's desk, drawing a pistol as he went.

Benton, restrained by another senator had turned back toward his seat. Perceiving the pistol he turned, tore open his coat and shirt and yelled, "I am not armed . . . let him fire . . . let the assassin fire." Turmoil ensured. When order was restored, Benton again shouted that a pistol had been brought in to assassinate him. Foote claimed self-defense because of a threat to shoot him.

Dickinson plucked the pistol from Foote's hand and locked it in his desk. The Senate, its dignity affronted, appointed a committee to look into the matter. No action was taken. News spread across the country and to Europe. The Senate's reputation suffered.[1]

Congressional Courtesy

Thaddeus Stevens, the acerbic congressman from Pennsylvania, was making a speech, when a colleague asked him to yield. He declined and did so again as the second request was made. At the third interruption, he reluctantly yielded the floor, saying, "My colleague will now make a few feeble remarks."[2]

Certain courtesy is required in the British House of Commons, as well, though it seems scarce when the Prime Minister is being questioned. An M.P. cannot call another member a liar. Churchill got around the rule by accusing a colleague of uttering a "terminological inexactitude." By the time everyone figured it out, it was too late to rebuke him.

[1] Nevins, Allen, *Ordeal of the Union*, New York, Charles Scribner's Sons, 1947.
[2] Owsley Lecture in a Vanderbilt graduate course.

A Swarm of Locusts

The Homestead Act of 1862 provided 160 acres of land to Americans who would settle on the tract and cultivate it for five years. As pioneers streamed into the Western plains they discovered a host of problems—lack of timber to build houses, for firewood, no material for fences, and worst of all, hordes of locusts.

The settlers made makeshift fences in two ways. They built sod fences, using a special plow which turned a four-inch layer of sod, more than a foot-wide, upside down. Then a similar layer from the other side fell on top. After that, sections of sod like building blocks were laid on top, overlapping the joints. Some made fences of the maclura plant or osage orange, that is, hedges of this thorny bush. Barbed wire was to come later.

Instead of wood, people on the plains burned hanks of prairie grass, in special stoves, and built houses out of sod. One might travel several miles to secure limbs to use as poles across the roof to support the sod. Now let us consider the other problem—the "Rocky Mountain Locusts."

These voracious grasshoppers, traveling in numbers that darkened the sky, had appeared along the Missouri river in the 1850s. In the decades following they reappeared from time to time. The worst plague came in 1874 surpassing any grasshopper attacks before or after. They rode the high winds from the north. The settlers on the Great Plains called it "the grasshopper year."

The spring and summer of the grasshopper year was good for growing crops. Wheat and oats were being gathered and put in shocks. Then farmers noticed a dark cloud approaching, but instead of a summer squall, it was a moving mass of locusts, borne by the wind. They descended on the land, piled up several inches deep, and began to eat everything in sight. The grain in the shock disappeared under the relentless attack of the hungry insects. One farmer had a field of onions whose green tops soon disappeared. Then they started in on the bulbs. He was left with neat rows of holes where the onions had been. Some declared that they were overwhelmed with the rank onion breath of the grasshoppers as they flew overhead. Their lighting on the roofs of houses sounded like hail. Limbs broke from their weight.

The locust plague had a powerful effect on the livestock. Chickens, and turkeys, greedy eaters as they are, stuffed themselves with the insects. One farmer reported that he fattened a herd of hogs and a flock of chickens on grasshoppers. But the effect of the locust plague on farmers was devastating. They tied string around their pants legs to keep out the insects and watched in futile silence while their crops were devoured.

The grasshopper invasion was not local, but reached from the Dakotas to Texas and East to Missouri. Grasshoppers piled up on railroad tracks to the point that Union Pacific trains were stopped. Rolling over piles of grasshoppers left such an oily mess that locomotives could not get traction to move. Section hands were called in to shovel the piles of insects off the tracks.

Locust plagues are not restricted to the past. They create a major problem today in the Mideast and Africa. One of the problems related to the famine in Niger, in 2005 was a plague of locusts.

Dick, Everett, *The Sod-House Frontier*, New York, D. Appleton Century Co., 1937.

The Indispensable Yam

The sweet potato, or yam, has ranked next to corn in Southern diet across the centuries. They are served roasted, fried, candied, or in custard pies. This staple of the Southern table comes in many shades and varieties, from rich orange when baked, to creamy white. A sweet potato may weigh from a quarter of a pound up to five pounds. The choice ones are smooth, red, and weigh three to the pound.

On our South Alabama farm we would grow an acre or so, yielding many bushels, to last through the winter. You let sweet potatoes sprout shoots, called slips, and plant a row or two of slips about three feet apart. These quickly produce vines which are then pruned to provide cuttings about a foot long. The ends of these are pressed into the ground using a notched stick. They soon form roots. This is the way the main crop is started.

Children on the farm could hardly wait for the first potatoes to mature If you saw a crack in the ground near the base of the vine you would feel around in the loose soil with your fingers (called grabbling) find a tuber and pull it out, leaving the plant intact to produce more. One plant would have several potatoes attached to its roots.

The potatoes were plowed up in the fall, gathered by children, and hauled to the farm house for storage. We had a small log barn called "the potato house." Inside, it was dug below ground level. Bushels of potatoes would be placed on a bed of pine straw, covered with more pine straw, then more potatoes, and so on. It took a lot to last all winter. Small tubers and vines were fed to the live-stock.

An article in a Mississippi newspaper in 1841 makes clear how indispensable the yam really was:

A traveler in Southeastern Mississippi stopped one night at a lonely farm where the provender for his horse was a trough of sweet potatoes and a rack filled with their dried vines. At supper a roast fowl was stuffed with sweet potatoes, a hash of wild turkey had them intermixed, flanking platters offered sweet potatoes baked and fried, others were in the biscuit and in the pie, and a decoction of dried sweet potatoes was drunk instead of coffee. After a glass of potato beer the guest went to bed. Next morning he had a sore throat which his hostess relieved with a hot potato poultice and a dose of potato vine tea.[1]

The writer may have been stretching truth a bit, but not much. We ate sweet potatoes every day and sometimes three times a day. A baked sweet potato, left over from dinner, was a favorite snack after school. Leftover, baked yams, sliced and fried in butter, is gourmet food. Modern health experts extol the nutritional benefits of sweet potatoes. With our diet of yams, corn bread, collards, and black-eyed peas, we ate better on the farm than we realized.

In World War II, a soldier, far from the rural south, entered a New York restaurant and ordered pie. The waitress asked what kind. The astonished soldier said, "Why, tater pie, of course. What other kind is they?"

In graduate school I wrote a paper on Voltaire's *Candide*. As I remember, fifty years later, the story ends with the main character, after a tempestuous life, settling down on a small farm to live in peace and grow vegetables. I wrote at the end of the paper, "Historians and philosophers have often wondered what kinds of vegetables were grown. I'm sure they were sweet potatoes—candide sweet potatoes." There was no response from the professor but I got a good grade on the course!

[1] J.F.R. Claiborne, *Natchez Free Trader and Daily Gazette*, December 21, 1841. Cited in Ulrich B. Phillips, *Life and Labor In the Old South,* Boston, Little, Brown and Co., 1935.

Malefactors of Great Wealth

There were many deplorable business practices in the late 1800s, before antitrust legislation began to restrict activity in the "Age of Big Business." One unscrupulous practice was to sell watered stock, that is, overstating the value of shares of stock. The term can be traced to cattle drovers like Daniel Drew.

Drew would manipulate the appetite and thirst of cattle on the way to market. Witholding food, he would give salt, and just before delivery would let the cattle fill up on water. A steer could drink an amount equal to 5 percent of its body weight. The butcher's scales recorded the water as though it were beef. Drew's biographer said that, though he had to deal with a different butcher each trip, "He took in profits with a big spoon."

Drew took his gain from selling cattle and went into Wall Street. He discovered that his unscrupulous practice would work in watering shares of stock before delivering it to the customer.[1]

Another unscrupulous practice was the forming of trusts in order to monopolize business. Corporations, unchecked by legislation, would ruthlessly drive competitors out of business. John D. Rockefeller, one of the better "masters of capital," once said, "We mean to control the coal oil business" and, for a time, Standard Oil did so.

Then came the Sherman Anti-Trust Act of 1890, making it illegal for any combination to act in restraint of trade. The legislation could be interpreted in different ways and clever lawyers got to work to find a way around the law. John G. Johnson, of Philadelphia, was retained by B.H. Harriman, one of those "malefactors of great wealth," used as a target by T.R. Roosevelt.

Harriman worked up one of his railroad mergers and wired it, in lengthy and minute detail to the lawyer. He wanted to know if the merger were possible and if it would violate the Sherman Anti-Trust Act. The answer came within twenty-four hours and it was four words long—"Merger possible; conviction certain." Johnson submitted a bill to Harriman for $100,000, $25,000 a word. This would be like a million dollars today.[2]

[1] White, Bouck, *The Book of Daniel Drew*, New York, George W. Doran Co., 1910.
[2] Fuller, Edmund, *Thesaurus of Anecdotes*, New York, Crown Publishers, 1942.

Sequel to Homestead

One of the labor disputes that reached crisis proportions was the Homestead Strike in 1892. Henry Frick, chairman of the Carnegie Steel Company, dealt with the labor union, The Amalgamated Association, on the matter of wage reduction, but no agreement was reached. Then the workers seized Carnegie property and when a private army of 300 Pinkerton guards was called in, war broke out. The guards were beaten up.

Several deaths resulted and the Pinkertons surrendered. Order was finally restored by the use of troops. Frick was severely criticized for the way he dealt with the union and public opinion turned against the steel company. Then something happened to change the criticism to sympathy and put the union in a bad light.

A criminal fanatic, a Russian anarchist named Berkman, came to Frick's office to kill the man who, he thought, represented the tyranny of capital. He had no connection with labor unions or with the Homestead mill. He shot Frick twice and stabbed him several times before Frick and staff members overpowered him. The police were called and the turmoil subsided. Frick then dictated two telegrams, one to Carnegie and one to his mother, "Was shot twice but not dangerously." To Carnegie's message he added his intent "to fight the battle out." Then he consented to let the surgeons probe for the bullets. He refused an anesthetic so he could assist the doctors, while conscious.

This completed, Frick returned to his desk, over protests of his staff, signed letters and dealt with several unfinished matters of business. Then he wrote a bulletin for the public stating his policy toward the union was unchanged. He said, "I do not think I will die, but if I do or not, the company will pursue the same policy and it will win." Then a stretcher was brought and he was taken home.

During recovery he continued his work, a telephone nearby, and two or three secretaries at this bedside. The public was fascinated.

Three weeks after the assassination attempt, Frick arose, ate breakfast, hopped a streetcar, and went back to his desk. The antagonism directed toward Frick changed to sympathy and admiration for his coolness and courage. It was disastrous for the Amalgamated Association. O'Donnell, the union leader said, "The bullet from Berkman's pistol went straight through the heart of the Homestead strike."[1]

Workers flooded in from all over the country to fill the vacancies, as well as former workers, ignoring the rules of union membership. The union surrendered and organized labor, in the steel industry, had to wait until the 1930s to gain any victories.

[1] Hendrick, Burton J., *The Life of Andrew Carnegie*, Garden City, Doubleday, Doran and Co., 1932.

IV
The Civil War

The Road to the Civil War

When the issue of admitting Missouri as a slave state arose in 1818, a political explosion occurred. It sounded an alarm "Like a fire-bell in the night," as Jefferson put it. This would upset the balance between slave and free states. The issue was settled in 1820 and the balance continued by admitting Maine as a free state and Missouri as slave, as well as providing that all states admitted in the future, North of 36° 30′, would be free. The nation heaved a sigh of relief over the Missouri Compromise.

Tensions began to mount again when the Abolitionist attack against slavery, led by Garrison, Weld, and the Grimke sisters, began about 1830. At that point, southerners who had considered it a necessary evil, began to defend the "peculiar institution."

Then the U. S. found itself with a vast new territory, a result of the war with Mexico. Then the admission of California as a free state became a heated issue. The Wilmot Proviso, which provided that all other states carved out of the Mexican Cession would be free, increased tensions. Secession threatened.

The whole matter came to a head in 1850 at a time when there were fifteen slave states balanced by fifteen free states. Great characters marched across the stage—Calhoun, the fiery Southerner, proponent of "nullification"; Clay, the "Great Pacificator"; and Webster, the strong unionist.

The debate continued for ten weeks with the state of the nation hanging in the balance. Leading northern Democrats, Webster and Douglas, were conciliatory. Webster so much so that Whittier's poem "Ichabod" had scathing lines of criticism. Whittier later expressed regret that he had been so harsh.

Then Clay offered a compromise that contained these provisions:

Admit California as a free state.

Enact a strict fugitive slave law (to please the South).

Abolish the slave trade in D.C.

Organize new territories in the Southwest without the Wilmot Proviso and providing for "popular sovereignty."

Adjust boundary between Texas and New Mexico.

The compromise was approved and a sigh of relief went up across the country. It was surprisingly well received in the South. The compromise was viewed as a final settlement and a good example of statesmanship.

During the debate an interesting drama had occurred. Before Webster made his famous "Seventh of March" speech, he visited the venerable Calhoun, thought to be on his deathbed. Calhoun expressed sadness that he was too ill to come to hear the speech. However as Webster was speaking Calhoun, a tall, gaunt figure, clad in black with a thick mane of white hair down to his shoulders, tottered into the chamber, unseen by the speaker, and with the assistance of other Senators, sank into his seat. Then Webster alluded to an utterance of the "distinguished Senator" from South Carolina, unable, because of illness to be present. Calhoun shifted restlessly and made as if to rise and interrupt the orator. The effort was too much for him and he sank back in his chair.

The speech continued and once again Webster quoted Calhoun and expressed regret over his absence. The ghostly figure, unable to bear the thought that he was considered absent, and half rising from his chair, Calhoun, in a feeble voice, yet one heard throughout the chamber, cried, "The Senator from South Carolina is in his seat."[1]

Webster turned with a start, and, perceived that his friend had defied death. Webster paused in his speech and showed deep emotion as he responded with a bow and a smile. Calhoun died a few days later.

Then came the Kansas-Nebraska Act of 1854, one of the most fateful measures ever passed by Congress. Douglas rammed through Congress a bill which would open the door for Kansas to be a slave state and Nebraska a free state. It was a reckless action, repealing the Compromise of 1820, violating the Compromise of 1850, and impelling the nation down the slippery steps toward war. Furthermore it shattered the Democratic Party and prepared the way for the rise of the Republican Party.

The extension of slavery into the territories was the principal issue leading to the Civil War. Undergirding this was the struggle between the sections for political power. The evils of the system of slavery were vividly portrayed in Stowe's *Uncle Tom's Cabin*, probably the most influential novel in the history of America.

[1] Harvey, Peter, *Reminiscences and Anecdotes of Daniel Webster*, Boston, Little Brown and Company, 1877.

Myths about Slavery

There are many misunderstandings about slaves and the system of American Negro slavery. This "peculiar institution" as some called it, was a burden to the conscience of Americans, including some slave-owners. To be fair, one must examine it in the light of its time. Here are some examples of myths about slavery, with comment:

Slaves were former naked savages.
On the contrary some, such as the Ashanti, represented a relatively high level of civilization with a system of taxation, courts of law, and an army.
The blame for slavery rests with Southern slave-owners.
There is enough blame to go around. It starts with African chiefs who captured natives from other tribes and held them in pens until they were sold. Guilt rests heavily on Arab slave-traders who treated the captives with great cruelty while on the way to river or seaports where blacks were sold to ship captains. These, often British, transported the Negroes, under inhumane conditions, to the Americas. Here they were worked in the fields and elsewhere on the farm.
Slavery was restricted to the South.
At the beginning of the Civil War there were 4 million slaves in America, 3.5 million of them in states that formed the Confederacy. Missouri had 115,000 slaves;

Arkansas, 111,000; and Maryland, 87,000. Smaller numbers were held by other border and northern states.

Slaves were mostly held on great plantations.

Not exactly. Most were owned by small farmers, with two to four slaves, and the farmer often worked alongside them in the field. Most southerners owned no slaves.

Slaves were brutally treated and beaten as a typical thing.

Slaves were valuable property, a prime field hand selling for, perhaps, ten times that of a prized horse. Thus their health was valued and they were well-fed. Even if kindly slave-owners treated slaves fairly, their bondage was a heavy burden to bear. Some slave-owners, in their wills, provided for the freeing of their slaves. There were about 500,000 free Negroes in America at the beginning of the Civil War.

President Lincoln looked on Negroes as brothers and equals.

He thought slavery was a sin but he did not think the black race equal to the white. Frederick Douglass called Lincoln "A genuine representative of American prejudice," but he came to appreciate him. Lincoln was the best friend the Negroes ever had.

White people were the slave-holders, period.

Over 3700 black slave-owners held over 3,000 slaves. In addition, the Cherokee Indians of Georgia were major slave owners.

The Emancipation Proclamation, in January, 1863, brought freedom to slaves in America.

It declared them free in states, held by Confederates, where it could not be enforced, and left them enslaved in the Border States where it could have been enforced. Slavery was still practiced in Delaware after the war. Lincoln compared his proclamation to the Pope's bull against the Comet. Still, it was a valuable propaganda influence and strengthened the moral cause of the Union. The Thirteenth Amendment, in 1865, ended slavery in America. However, Arkansas, Louisiana, Maryland, and Missouri had already abolished it.

Because of the demands of King Cotton, the U.S. was the chief importer of slaves.

Wrong. Less than 5% of slaves brought from Africa came to the U.S. The United States outlawed the importation of slaves in 1808. Brazil imported 4 million slaves and the Spanish empire, 2.5 million.

Slavery was the sole cause of the Civil War.

It was a major cause, especially the issue of extending it into the territories, but not the only one.

The strict New England conscience early perceived the moral wrong of slavery.

Not until slavery proved unprofitable. New England sea captains were prominent in the slave trade, one of the worst aspects of slavery.

It was inevitable that the Confederate states would lose their investment in slaves if they were defeated.

President Lincoln favored, until the end, compensated emancipation, and at the Hampton Roads Conference, in February, 1865, he proposed to set aside $400,000,000 to indemnify slave owners, if hostilities ceased. The Confederate commissioners were foolish not to accept it.

Slave owners often tore families apart and sold family members down the river.

Slave owners had economic incentives to keep families together and morals high.

Slaves were worked to the point of exhaustion.

Actually they were relatively well treated because of their value on the farm. One of the three slave-owners described in Stowe's *Uncle Tom's Cabin*, was cruel and the other two very kind, but the public remembered Simon Legree and forgot the others.

Slaves were the main sources of labor from the beginning of English settlements in this country.

White indentured servants furnished most of the labor in the 1600s. After the Asiento agreement in 1713 the English participated in the slave trade. However, slavery was not too popular and in fact, was diminishing in the late 1700s in the face of anti-slavery societies, many of them in the South. Eli Whitney's cotton gin changed this.

Prior to the Civil War each section was united: the North against slavery—the South for it.

It just seemed that way. The moderates on either side lost their voice. Unless one was vocally and extremely for or against slavery in either section he had little chance to be elected in the tense decade, prior to the war. Slavery was practiced in the North; in Indiana and Illinois until 1840, in Delaware until 1865.

The plantation system and slave-owning was the typical way of life in the South.

White population in 1860 was about 8 million. About 1/5th of the white families owned any slaves and only 8,000 owned 50 or more. Many of them were owned by yeoman farmers. Two thirds of white southerners had no direct connection with slavery.

Slaves tended to remain on the farm until the Civil War was over.

Many of the men left, some as servants to their masters who went off to war; others to fight in the Union Army. My great grandfather Spicer left Rose Hill, Alabama to fight for the Confederacy and never returned.

My grandmother, Luella Spicer Tipton, told of playing with slave children and eating her bread and milk with them at suppertime. Two negro women, twins, undertook the plowing, one leading the mule, the other holding the plow handles. Little Luella sat in a basket fastened to the plow-stock, a forerunner of such arrangement in grocery shopping carts.

Fogel, Robert W. and Engerman, Stanley L., *Time On The Cross*, New York, W. W. Norton and Co., 1974.
Stauffer, John, "Across the Great Divide," *Time*, July 4, 2005.
Shannon, Fred Albert, *America's Economic Growth*, Third Edition, New York, The Macmillan Company, 1951.
Fremont Wirth lectures at Peabody College.

Blacks as Slave-Owners

Americans have underestimated black people by not sufficiently recognizing that through diligence and the mercy of some slave-owners, prior to the Civil War, a considerable number of Negroes won their freedom and achieved prosperity. A number of free Negroes, particularly in Louisiana, Virginia, South Carolina, and Maryland, were well-to-do. Some owned plantations and, in 1830, there were 3,775 Negro owners, holding 12,907 slaves. Eighty-four was one of the largest numbers held by a black slave owner. Just before the war, Cyprien Ricard, of Louisiana, bought a plantation and 91 slaves for a quarter of a million dollars. Thomas Lafon, a colored merchant in New Orleans, died after the Civil War, leaving an estate of $500,000. Few people in the South were that rich. In today's economy that would probably total ten million dollars.[1]

In Louisiana, most of the wealthy colored people were mulattoes, who had been given a financial start by their white fathers.

Only 20 percent of the white people of the South owned slaves and most of them owned only one or two, and worked alongside them in the field.

The Cherokee Indians of Georgia owned slaves. Annie H. Able Henderson wrote a fascinating book on this topic, *The Slaveholding Indians of Georgia*.

You will notice that I have used different terms for black people, reflecting a wide range of current usage. We hear about the "United Negro College Fund" and the "National Association for the Advancement of Colored People," both alive and well. I understand Whoopi Goldberg's statement, "I'm not an African-American. I've never been to Africa." Where I was raised in South Alabama, it was polite to say "colored people."

Terminology is important and respect ought to attend any term used. When I was Dean of a Georgia college two black students came to protest a teacher's pronunciation of "negro." They didn't seem to object to the term except that he pronounced it "nigrah." They thought it was a plantation term; he maintained it was simply his southern accent. Impasse! I tried to ease the tension by expressing appreciation for one of the girl's father, whom I knew.

[1] Material drawn from Shannon, Fred Albert, *America's Economic Growth*, New York, MacMillan, 1951.

Foraging for Food

In the War Between the States soldiers in both the Confederate and Union armies were forced to forage the countryside for much of their food. These soldiers developed foraging into a fine art. While doubts are cast on the claim of some soldiers to be able to milk a cow through a crack of a fence while the farmer's wife, blissfully unaware, milked on the other side, it must be admitted that they were quite resourceful.

One squad of foragers, faced with a high fence which a farmer had cannily erected around his chicken pen, equipped themselves with fishing poles. They baited hook and line with grains of corn and took their position in some nearby bushes. The unsuspecting farmer was giving the chickens their late afternoon feeding when some of them, as well hooked as any sucker, rose up in the air, squawking and fluttering, to disappear over the fence.

Dr. Frank Owsley, history professor at Vanderbilt University in the 1940s, told this story, and many more good ones, I might add. I wanted to use it in my dissertation and wrote him to verify it. By this time he was at the University of Alabama. He wrote back to say that, "No one should hold an Owsley accountable for all his stories but that, yes, this was true." Then he went on to tell me another one.

His Uncle "Dink" Owsley, written up in a post-war novel, told of his foraging effort. He went to the backyard of a farm, cast a baited line and hooked a turkey gobbler. Hearing a door slam he ran around the house and down the road, the turkey trotting behind. The farmer's wife called after him, "Don't run, mister. That gobbler will chase you but he won't hurt you." Man and bird disappeared in a cloud of dust.[1]

The fine art of foraging was alive and well in World War II. In the South Pacific there was a continuing tension between sailors on ships and shore-based personnel. They skimmed off the best of the supplies. My sub-chaser, a very small ship, would requisition Campbell's soup—chicken and vegetable-beef. What we got was ox-tail and Scotch broth. The popular brands had been taken by the shore-based people, despite the Admiral's orders that preference should be given to small ships. The struggle was on! When I would take a work-party down the bay to the Navy Warehouse, one or two men would drift away to do some scouting. The rest would follow the clerk with the clipboard and the foragers would find choice items to slip into the boat. So far my conscience for this "moonlight requisition" has not bothered me.[2]

[1] Dr. Frank Owsley in "American Sections" class in 1948, and in a letter dated 1/16/1953.
[2] Personal observation.

Stonewall Jackson and What He Ate

General Stonewall Jackson was such a brilliant military leader that his tactics in the valley campaign in 1861–62 were still being studied in war colleges in the twentieth century.

He also had some peculiar personality traits. For example, when he was teaching mathematics at Virginia Military Institute, he would sit in a chair, facing a blank wall, and mentally project problems for the next day's lessons, and work through them, looking at the wall.

He was concerned about his digestion and, when at home, allowed a "quiet time" after each meal, to allow his food to digest. When in the field his appetite sometimes got him in trouble. Near a persimmon tree laden with ripe fruit, he stopped his troops, dismounted, climbed the tree and ate his fill. Then he found he couldn't get down. (spurs interfering, no doubt). His men pulled rails from a nearby fence extended them into the tree and "skidded" him down.

Another time he couldn't resist a thicket of ripe blackberries. Though a battle was going on nearby, he was out in the patch, with his aide, eating the ripe berries. Then he paused and asked a philosophical, and also anatomical, question, "If you had a choice, about where to be wounded, where would you prefer to be hit?" The aide, mindful of bullets hitting all around, replied, "I'd rather not be hit in the blackberry patch!"[1]

Jackson and his army would fight all day and march all night to catch the enemy by surprise next morning, twenty miles away. On the move General Jackson would nap in the saddle. A soldier spotted him, slouched in the saddle, swaying precariously, and called out, "Old Fellow, where the—did you get your licker?" The General roused up, and was recognized by the dumbfounded soldier. This Johnny Reb exclaimed, "It's Old Jack," jumped the fence and found cover.[2]

General Jackson was mistakenly shot by his own troops after a night reconnaissance during the Battle of Chancellorsville in 1862. The last words from this deeply religious man before he died were, "Let us cross over the river and rest under the trees." General Lee's response to Jackson's death was, "I have lost my right arm."

[1] Henderson, G. F. R., *Stonewall Jackson and the American Civil War*, New York, Grosset and Dunlap.
[2] Wiley, Bell Irvin, *The Life of Johnny Reb*, New York, The Bobbs-Merrill Co., 1943.

Climbing Missionary Ridge

In November, 1863, General Grant confronted General Bragg in the three-day battle of Lookout Mountain—Missionary Ridge. Bragg's army occupied the top of the mountain in heavily fortified positions. The battle on November 25 was not going well for the Union and two of General Thomas' divisions moved out to attack the rifle pits at the foot of Missionary Ridge. This was only to relieve pressure on General Sherman. To everyone's amazement, Union troops carried the rifle pits and fought their way up the steep mountain side, practically chinning themselves on tree limbs. The sudden unorthodox attack surprised the Confederates, firmly entrenched at the crest, to the point of panic. A position was given away which should have been easy to defend. General Bragg wrote to President Jefferson Davis expressing his "shameful discomfiture" with the action at Chattanooga. J.G. Randall said, "It was a sudden impulse which no commander could have either created or restrained."[1]

While Grant was demanding of his generals "Who ordered this attack?" Union troops were routing the Confederates at the top. General Granger, without much foresight, threatened to court-martial the troops for disobeying orders and taking the whole mountain, instead of just the rifle pits. It didn't happen.

I taught American history for decades, and always took note of the mystery of the spontaneous mountainside attack. Then I read Douglas MacArthur's *Reminiscences*, in which he declares that his father, Arthur MacArthur, a Colonel at age nineteen, inspired the troops, led the attack, and carried the mountaintop.[2]

The victory at Chattanooga helped ease the humiliation of the Confederate victory at Chickamauga.

When the South was divided into military districts during reconstruction, and ruled by major-generals, it was dangerous to exhibit Confederate sympathies. At a celebration of the Union victory, a die-hard son of the South kept yelling "You won the war but we whipped you at Chickamauga." An officer rode up to him and threatened dire punishment. The unrepentant rebel changed sides and started yelling "We won the war but you sure whipped us at Chickamauga."

[1] Randall, J. G., *The Civil War and Reconstruction*, page 5, New York, D. C. Heath and Company, 1937.

[2] MacArthur, Douglas, *Reminiscences*, New York, McGraw-Hill Book Company, 1964.

Historical Snapshots—The Civil War

Feelin' for a Furlough

How to deal with fear in time of battle is an issue for every soldier in every war. I found, in World War II, that the greatest deterrent to giving way to fear was concerns over what one's comrades would think. Peer pressure is at work along with one's desire to do his duty.

During the War Between the States, as battle raged, an officer asked a soldier why he was behind a tree waving his arms on either side. He replied, "I'm feelin' for a furlough." He was seeking a slight wound which would permit him to go home.[1]

Fraternization during the Civil War

It is difficult to understand how soldiers from North and South could fight so fiercely in great battles like Gettysburg and Cold Harbor, and then be so friendly between battles. They traded clothes, tobacco, and coffee, and did a little visiting between the lines.

The Battle of Murfreesboro, in the last day of 1862 and the first three days in 1863, was a major conflict with over 30,000 men on each side. On the night before the battle, the band of the Union Army played northern favorites while the Confederates listened. Then the Confederate band played tunes that were favorites in the South. Finally, both bands joined in to play "Home Sweet Home." Then soldiers on both sides began to sing, swelling the chorus on the clear wintry air. I would guess that some tears were shed by homesick soldiers.[2]

Night Raid to Memphis

General Nathan Bedford Forrest, who was supposed to use "Fustest With the Mostest" as a formula for military success, relied on surprise and the ability to make the enemy think he had the most. He was giving Union forces a hard time, in 1864, as he roamed over Mississippi. Sherman sent Smith and Mower south with 17,000 men to corner Forrest and his 5,000.

Knowing he could not prevail in open battle, Forrest took 2,000 men and attacked Memphis, held by Union forces for two years. At three o'clock on a Sunday, August morning, stealing through a thick fog, he struck a devastating blow at the Union military. The Confederates failed to capture the three Union generals known to be in Memphis, though one escaped in his nightshirt, his

84

pants a prize of war. It was reported that Forrest had a new union uniform tailor-made and sent with apologies for the tactless behavior of his men.[3] As expected, the Smith column was recalled to protect the base in Memphis.

Luxury Prison and Others

Have you ever heard of prisoners of war being housed in a luxury hotel? Consider the historic Maxwell House Hotel in Nashville. It was built in 1859 by Judge John Overton who was supposed to have bought the lot for $115, by mistake, at an auction. It was so big and grand that, in the early years it was dubbed "Overton's folly."

Federal troops occupied Nashville in 1862, and made the hotel a prison for Confederate soldiers. Unfortunately, prisoners descended a temporary stairway from the fifth to the first floor for breakfast and it collapsed. Forty-five men were killed and ninety-two were injured.

Southern prisons were far from being luxurious. In fact Andersonville and Belle Isle were disgraceful, being more like concentration camps. Those in charge were overwhelmed by the numbers, 35,000 at Andersonville, alone, on sixteen acres of land. They did see that the prisoners received the same rations as the soldiers who guarded them. Many captured Confederates were housed in existing forts and prisons. Disease was a major problem. My great-grandfather Spicer, from Rose Hill, Alabama, was sent to Elmira Prison in New York, where he died of typhoid fever.

Not counting those paroled on the field, the Confederates took 195,000 prisoners; the Union, 215,000.[4]

Fighting Joe Wheeler

During the Spanish-American War "Fighting Joe" Wheeler, a youthful Confederate general in the Civil War, volunteered for service. The press made much of his exchange of Confederate gray for Union blue. In the battle of Las Guasimas, his troops came under heavy fire. He led an attack, and the Spanish began to flee. The old, white-bearded warrior rose up in his stirrups, waved his saber, and with understandable lapse of memory, yelled, "Come on boys, we've got the Yankees on the run."[5]

Shot in the Wooden Leg

In the Battle of Gettysburg in Pennsylvania, in July, 1863, part of the bitter fighting was around Evergreen Cemetery, where signs warned against fireworks. Two confederate generals were examining the position, pending an effort to seize it. A mini ball whistled through the air and struck Ewell with a thud. He said to General Gordon, "Suppose the ball had struck you; we would have had the trouble of carrying you off the field. It doesn't hurt a bit to be shot in a wooden leg."[6]

It is amazing how officers continued to fight though wounded or crippled. John B. Hood stayed in action after losing a leg and the use of an arm. When Nathan Bedford Forrest was shot in the leg and unable to ride a horse, he stayed in the field, riding in a buggy with foot propped on the dashboard, and a pistol in his hand.

[1] Wiley, Bill Irvin, *The Life of Johnny Reb*, New York, The Bobbs-Merrill Company, 1943.
[2] Foote, Shelby, *The Civil War*, *Fredericksburg to Meridian*, New York, Random House, 1963.
[3] Henry, Robert Self, *The Story of the Confederacy*, New York, The Bobbs-Merrill Company, 1943.

[4] Randall, J. G., *The Civil War and Reconstruction*, Boston, D.C. Heath and Company, 1937.
[5] Millis, Walter, *The Martial Spirit*, Boston, Houghton Mifflin Company, 1931.
[6] Henry, Robert Selph, *The Story of the Confederacy*, New York, The Bobbs-Merrill Company, 1943.

The Strange Election of 1864

Prospects were grim for President Lincoln's re-election in 1864. The war had been running downhill, with General Grant bogged down in the "Wilderness" campaign in Virginia and Sherman's army before Atlanta. The country was tired of the war. Salmon P. Chase opined that a different man was needed for the presidency for the next four years and made it clear that he, the Secretary of the Treasury, was that man. He encouraged his friends to organize a campaign for him. When it became known, he denied it.

The "Radical Republicans" conspired against Lincoln and tried to postpone the national convention, hoping that further military losses would turn the country against the President. These dissident Republicans, "The Radical Democracy," as they named themselves, called a special convention in Cleveland, and nominated John Fremont. The success of the Convention was not overwhelming. Only four hundred people showed up. When Lincoln heard about it, he laughed, and read from the Bible:

> And every one in distress, and every one that was in debt, and every one that was discontented, gathered themselves unto him and he became a captain over them; and there were with him about four hundred men.

Then Lincoln did an unusual thing, acting as a superb politician, according to my old Vanderbilt professor, Dr. Frank Owsley. He put the Republican Party on the shelf and ran on The Constitutional Union Party ticket. Who would vote against the Constitution and the Union? Well, many did.

Republican politicians, and newspapermen, led by Horace Greeley, banded together and tried to get him to withdraw, even after he was nominated. Greeley declared, "Mr. Lincoln is already beaten. He cannot be elected." Lincoln's supporters were uneasy and the chairman of the National Republican Committee gloomily said to Lincoln, "The tide is against us." Lincoln had going for him the adage "Don't change horses in the middle of the stream."

Lincoln prepared himself for defeat and had his cabinet sign a statement that they would support the new president-elect, as he would.

The Democrats nominated General George McClellan, the reluctant warrior. The platform called for "the immediate cessation of hostilities . . . at the earliest practicable moment." McClellan accepted the nomination but rejected the platform, a first and last action of its type.

But the tide turned, contrary to the Republican National Committee chairman's prediction. Sherman conquered Atlanta and Farragut triumphed at Mobile Bay. The President's detractors climbed on his band wagon, including Chase and Greeley. Lincoln won the election overwhelmingly, 2,213,665 popular votes to McClellan's 1,802,237.

Ralph Waldo Emerson wrote "Seldom in history was so much staked on a popular vote. I suppose never in history." Lincoln thought that the election, even with the strife, was good for the country. He said, "It has demonstrated that a people's government can sustain a national election in the midst of a great civil war." He had a bright hope that the nation would soon be united again. His dream for his beloved nation was cut short by John Wilkes Booth.

Lectures by Dr. Frank Owsley in the "American Sections" course at Vanderbilt University.
Lorant, Stefan, *The Life of Abraham Lincoln*, New York, A Mentor Book, 1954.

Abraham Lincoln—Appearance and Substance

Abraham Lincoln was a homely man. He was six feet, four inches tall and weighed about one hundred eighty pounds when elected President in 1860. He had narrow shoulders, and was thin and wiry. He had long arms, big hands, large ears, and a kind of leathery look to his skin. At first glance he looked frail but he was a powerful man, a skilled wrestler and one who could lift four hundred pounds. Five photographs in 1860 show sunken cheeks and deep-set eyes. His law partner said that "Melancholy dripped from him." After he took the advice of an eleven year-old girl and grew a beard, the first president to do so, he looked less hollow-cheeked.

In his early years, in rural Illinois, he was driving a wagon and overtook a farm woman carrying a load. Responding to his invitation, she climbed into the wagon. Then looking him full in the face she said, with frontier candor, "You are the ugliest man I ever saw." To this Lincoln replied, "Well, there is not much I can do about that." She answered, "Oh yes there is. You could stay at home."

Hidden beneath this rugged exterior was a keen mind and strong character, revealed in the following traits and characteristics:

Political skill, shown in the election of 1864, capacity for daring decisions, as in proclaiming the Emancipation Proclamation, his charity toward the defeated South, and his gifted use of the English language. We consider these to be indicators of a great man.

He was eloquent in speech and writing. Every schoolchild is acquainted with the great Gettysburg Address, ill-perceived at the time, but whose soaring words have echoed across the decades. His First Inaugural Address has noble phrases also. When you read his appeal to the South you feel the impact:

> I am loath to close. We are not enemies but friends. We must not be enemies. Though passion has strained, it must not break our bonds of affection. The mystic chords of memory, stretching from every battlefield, and patriot grave, to every living heart and hearthstone, all over this broad land, will yet swell the chorus of the Union, when again touched, as surely they will be, by the better angels of our nature.

Stefan Lorant called it "a prose of Biblical beauty."

Lorant, Stefan, *The Life of Abraham Lincoln*, New York, Mentor Books, 1954.
Randall, J. G., *The Civil War and Reconstruction*, Boston, D.C. Heath and Company, 1937.

Lincoln Anecdotes

Abraham Lincoln was such an interesting character that many anecdotes about him are available and numerous quotations are attributed to him, too many, perhaps.

A small book has been written about things Lincoln did not say, that are attributed to him.

Here are some of my favorite anecdotes about "The Great Emancipator."

Emancipation Proclamation

President Lincoln planned to release the proclamation earlier but delayed until there was an appropriate Union victory. The Battle of Antietam in October, 1862, passed as the achievement he was looking for, and he made the announcement in January, 1863. It declared the slaves free in the Confederate states where it could not be enforced, and left them untouched, in the border states where it could have been effected. He doubted his constitutional authority to free slaves except as to count them as property seized from the enemy. He likened his action to the Pope's bull against the comet. It did give the union higher moral ground and helped its standing in Europe.

Red-Hot Stove

Thaddeus Stevens, sharp-tongued member of the House of Representatives, was asked about Simon Cameron, by President Lincoln. The President was considering appointing Cameron to high office. Stevens was reluctant to recommend him and Lincoln said, "You don't mean to say that Cameron would steal?" The acerbic Pennsylvanian's answer was, "No, I don't think he would steal a red-hot stove."

Lincoln loved a joke and this was funny to him. He repeated it, Cameron heard about it, and was highly incensed. He demanded a retraction. Stevens agreed to do this and said, "I retract it. Maybe he would steal a red-hot stove."

Cameron was appointed Secretary of War but he was so incompetent that Lincoln soon replaced him with Stanton.[1]

Reluctant Generals

During the Civil War, President Lincoln had difficulty finding an effective general for the Army of the Potomac. Neither Hooker nor Burnside (he of the famous sideburns) was successful. Then he appointed General Pope who didn't do much but indicated great activity by signing reports "Headquarters in the saddle." Lincoln read the report and said, "The trouble is that General Pope has his headquarters where his hindquarters ought to be."[2]

Generals and Mules

During the Civil War, a courier came dashing across the Long Bridge in Washington bearing the news that there was a Rebel raid at Falls Church, a dozen miles away. They had captured a Brigadier General and twelve Army mules. President Lincoln was upset. He exclaimed, "How unfortunate. I can fill his place with one of my generals, in five minutes, but those mules cost us two hundred dollars apiece."[3]

Lincoln Remembers

One of the traits that endeared Abraham Lincoln to Americans was his regard for the common man. As President he held receptions on Saturday, and people of every description came, some wearing hickory shirts and cowhide boots. Time and again he would remember people whom he had not seen in years. One such incident had its beginning in the period when he was young in politics.

In 1834 when he was a candidate for the legislature he called on a farmer to ask for his vote. He found him cutting hay and while he was presenting his cause the dinner bell rang. The farmer invited him for dinner but he declined, saying he would stay and mow a round or two. When the farmer returned he found three rows mowed and the scythe leaning against the gatepost. Almost thirty years later the old farmer and his wife attended a reception and stood in line to shake hands with the President. He recognized them, called them by name, and drew them aside for a talk. They were amazed that he remembered their name. He went on to mention mowing the hay, back there in Illinois.

The farmer said, "That is so" and mentioned the scythe left leaning on the gatepost. He went on to say that he wanted to ask a question that had been on his mind all these years: "What did you do with the whetstone?"

The President pushed his hair back and thought for a moment. Then his face lighted up. He acknowledged that he remembered and said, "I put it on the high gatepost." The farmer went home and found it on the post, where it had been for about thirty years.[4]

[1] Quoted portions are from Samuel W. McCall, *"Thaddeus Stevens,"* Boston, Houghton, Mifflin and Co., 1899.

[2] Owsley lectures at Vanderbilt University, 1948–49.

[3] Schuyler, Colfax, *Reminiscences of Abraham Lincoln, North American Review*, 1888.

[4] Coleman, Edna W., *Seventy-five Years of White House Gossip*, New York, Doubleday Page and Co., 1925.

The Civil War—The First Modern War

The Civil War, also called the "War Between the States," and by some termed "The War For Southern Independence" was notable for the numbers engaged, over 2 million (Union) and 900,000 (Confederates). The number of casualties was staggering—625,000. If those who died later of their wounds were counted, perhaps 1,000,000 died, more Americans lost than in any other war.

There were features of the war not seen in any previous conflict—the use of railroads, the telegraph, the Gatling gun (early machine gun), steel ships, submarines, and new repeating rifles. Some suggest the observation balloon, but these were used in the Napoleonic wars.

Railroads

Two-thirds of the total of the 30,000 miles of railroads were in the North. Railroads were used for shipping goods and men but more went by horse, wagon, and on foot.

A good example of the value of railroad transportation is found in the movement of Confederate forces after their defeat in the Battle of Shiloh in April, 1862. General Bragg fell back to Corinth, Mississippi, loaded the troops on trains which took them to Montgomery and from there to Chattanooga. Within three days they were ready for action again. I cannot think of any other brilliant action performed by General Bragg.

The Telegraph

President Lincoln seemed to rely on wire reports about military actions more than the Confederate President. He didn't like most of the reports he got. President

Lincoln tried to direct the war, personally, through the telegraph and other means. Perhaps this was because he lacked confidence in his General-in-Chief, first, Winfield Scott, and later Halleck. He finally found a general he could trust and turned the direction of military actions over to General Grant.[1]

Steel Ships

The U.S.S. *Constitution* was dubbed "Old Ironsides," in the War of 1812, because cannon balls bounced off her stout oaken sides. In the Civil War real iron-sided ships came into action.

The most notable engagement was between the *Monitor* (Union) and the *Merrimack* (Confederate). The *Merrimack* was a wooden ship which had iron plates added to its sides, and an iron ram built onto its prow. This ship, re-named *Virginia*, quickly destroyed the *Cumberland* and the *Congress* and threw consternation into Washington and the cities of the East Coast.

Then the *Monitor* appeared. It was a strange vessel, designed by a brilliant engineer, John Ericsson. It was a small ship, all-steel, its deck almost awash. With its rounded tower, with a port, through which two eleven-inch cannons could revolve in all directions, it looked like "a cheese-box on a raft." The two ships fought a naval duel on March 9, 1862 at close quarters below Fort Monroe. The result was inconclusive, as each withdrew without much damage. The *Virginia* was later destroyed to keep it from falling into the hands of the enemy.[2]

Submarines

Submarines have been around a long time. David Bushnell introduced one named the *Turtle* in the American Revolution. In the Civil War one was actually put to use. This was a small, cylindrical craft, powered by foot pedals, and moving very slowly. As many as twenty-four crew members took turns at the laborious task of manning the pedals.

The Confederate submarine, *Hunley* had a long spur, up forward, with an explosive attached. The idea was to ram a ship and sink it. The hope was that the blockade could be broken with this device.

On February 17, 1864, the *Hunley* with a crew of nine, moved out of Charleston Harbor and rammed the Union ship *Housatonic*. Rammed in the side, the ship sank, but so did the *Hunley*. The shock was too great. In 2004 the *Hunley* was raised and the remains of the Confederate sailors given a military funeral.[3]

New Rifles

Both sides had new, repeating rifles, many of them imported from England. Dr. Frank Owsley, Vanderbilt professor, noted that General Pemberton, who surrendered Vicksburg, July 4, 1863, had just received 1,200 new Enfield rifles. Knowing he was going to surrender, he should have dropped them down an old well instead of turning them over to General Grant. Some were of such superior quality that Union soldiers exchanged their rifles for those stacked in surrender. Incidentally, Pemberton was able to persuade Grant to change his "unconditional surrender" demand to parole for Confederate soldiers.[4]

Gatling Gun

This was the early version of the machine gun. It had a cluster of barrels, each one firing as it revolved.

It was designed by Richard J. Gatling (1818–1903), an American inventor. This weapon had limited use in the Civil War, though General Butler used two Gatling guns at Petersburg and eight on gun boats. A similar weapon was the revolving shotgun, used in the "taming of the west" in later decades.

The Gatling gun was hand-cranked, with six revolving barrels, and a hopper on top from which cartridges were fed. The gun could fire an astonishing 600 rounds per minute.

Gatling presented an improved, 1865 model, to the Ordnance Department which tested it. It used rim fire, copper-cased cartridges. It was adopted officially in 1866.[5]

The machine gun has played a major role in every war since. On my little ship, a Sub-chaser, in World War II, we had a permanently-mounted 20 millimeter, and air-cooled 50 and 30-caliber guns as needed. I prefer the 30-caliber. It doesn't give you a headache after you fire it for a while.

[1] Frank Owsley lectures at Vanderbilt University.

[2] Randall, J. G., *The Civil War and Reconstruction*, New York, D.C. Heath and Company, 1937.

[3] A narration by Bruce Cotton, American Heritage Publishing Company, 1960. See also, Alexander, W. A., The Confederate Submarine Torpedo Boat, "Hunley," *Gulf States Historical Magazine*, 1902. Another source is Garrison, Villard Oswald, "The Submarine and the Torpedo In the Blockade of the Confederacy," *Harpers Magazine*, 1916.

[4] Foote, Shelby, *The Civil War, Fredericksburg To Meridian*, and *Red River to Appomattox*, New York, Random House, 1974.

[5] *Historical Times Encyclopedia of the Civil War*, Boatner's *Civil War Dictionary*, and Edwards, *Civil War Guns*.

V

The Twentieth Century

Altercations in the Orient

The Spanish-American War, fought in the spring and early summer of 1898, was one conflict that should never have occurred. But America was in a warlike mood. The Monroe Doctrine had warned European powers not to colonize in this hemisphere. McKinley, unlike Cleveland, was unable to resist the urgings of the "Yellow Press," and individuals like Theodore Roosevelt were thirsting for action and glory. Moreover Spain did some stupid things in Cuba, though they didn't sink the battleship *Maine*. And so we went to war.

Along with action in Cuba and Puerto Rico, a decisive battle was fought in Manila Bay, in the Philippines. On May 1, Commodore George Dewey sailed into the Bay with four cruisers, and engaged Admiral Montojo's six antiquated ships. By noon every Spanish vessel was captured or sunk. Dewey lost only one man, from sunstroke. Then insurrection broke out in the islands, and Dewey was hard-pressed to resist forces led by Emilio Aguinaldo. Finally McKinley sent an expeditionary force, which paused on the way, to annex Guam. Manila finally surrendered on August 13. Dewey was a hero and America was elated over the success of a short war.

Later, General Arthur MacArthur was made military governor and continued the struggle with Aguinaldo. But the American way is to replace military with civilian administration. In 1900 William Howard Taft arrived to take charge as commissioner, and to win over "our little brown brothers" with kindness. MacArthur so resented his coming that he refused to go down to the ship to meet him and assigned him a small room. Taft made peaceful overtures and reminded the General that he would still be in command of the military, and exercise great power. To this MacArthur peevishly replied that this would be satisfactory except that he had been exercising much more power before Taft came.

Washington stood behind Taft and in 1901 MacArthur was relieved of his command. Civil authority had won out over the military. The General returned to America, went public and made some inflammatory public statements. President Theodore Roosevelt gave a strong protest about soldiers getting involved in politics and opined that such an officer was not fit to hold a commission in the National Guard.

Now, please fast-forward a half-century. The Korean War started in 1950 with the invasion of South Korea by the Communist North. The U.N. Security Council passed a resolution, during Russia's boycott, to approve U.N. intervention. The U.S. objective was to drive the North Korean forces back across the 38th parallel. General Douglas MacArthur was in command. He had a formidable foe, Russian-trained troops equipped with Russian tanks. After a brilliant landing at Inchon, in September, MacArthur pushed across the 38th parallel and captured

Pyongyang, the North Korean capital. Resistance collapsed and American forces rolled North on a broad front, toward the Yalu River. The Joint Chiefs of Staff advised MacArthur to hold up, but he pressed on. (In his *Reminiscences* MacArthur said he had their approval.) Warnings were ignored and the Chinese Army attacked with devastating force. By January of 1951, U.N. troops were pushed back to the 38th parallel.

Then MacArthur, irked by the restraints on him, went public with complaints about the Administration's policy. In so doing he challenged the constitutional principle of civilian authority over the military and, like his father, he lost. The straw that broke the camel's back was his ringing endorsement of an inflammatory speech criticizing the President by House Minority Leader, Joe Martin. The General's letter approving Martin's angry rhetoric made headlines all over the world. The British and other members of the U.N. Coalition expressed their wrath against MacArthur. President Truman recalled him in April, 1951.

The message relieving him of his command, written by George Marshall, was abrupt and gruff. It was an unceremonious dismissal, the way President Truman wanted it. MacArthur returned to the hysterical praise of the American public. When the news broke that MacArthur was fired my high school history class rose up with deep emotion to support MacArthur. This was typical all over the U.S. After Senate hearings, his popularity declined a bit. Thus ends the tale of two generals, father and son, brilliant officers who, after an altercation in the Orient, just "faded away."

General Douglas MacArthur had two brilliant achievements. As he recaptured Philippine territory in 1945 he would turn each town or province over to locals to govern. This did not meet the approval of some in Washington, but it made the Philippines love him. Perhaps his greatest achievement was guiding Japan from autocracy to democracy in the post-war period and helping them write a constitution. His imperial nature and long experience in the Orient made him an ideal military governor at that time.

The original objective of "containment," that is pushing the Communist forces back across the 38th parallel and bolstering the Republic of Korea army, was achieved. We won the war. In any war, changing objectives after the battle is begun is fraught with danger and disappointment.

Rovere, Richard R. and Schlesinger, Arthur M., Jr., New York, *The General and the President*, Farrar, Strauss, and Young, 1951.
Baldwin, Leland D. and Kelley, Robert, *The Stream of American History*, New York, third edition, American Book Company, 1965.
MacArthur, Douglas, *Reminiscences*, New York, McGraw-Hill Book Co., 1964.
Manchester, William, *American Caesar, Douglas MacArthur*, Boston, Little, Brown and Co., 1978.

Eager Warrior; Unconventional President

Theodore Roosevelt was a unique character, before his presidency, during, and after. He lived a rugged life on a cattle ranch, developing a strong body after a sickly childhood. He was police commissioner in New York in the 1890s. That was where he first met Booker T. Washington, who was carrying two suitcases down the street, late at night, on his way to a hotel. Roosevelt stepped up to help and carried one of the cases for him. They became friends.

As Assistant Secretary of the Navy he swung into action one afternoon when Secretary Long left him in charge. He sent messages to the Orient, putting the Navy on a war footing. When war did come in April, 1898 after the battleship *Maine* was sunk and Spain blamed, he and Col. Leonard Wood formed a regiment of volunteers, the "Rough Riders." These cowboys and college students went off to war, bursting with nationalism. From this time on you hear more about Roosevelt than Wood.

The regular army took a dim view of these untrained volunteers and tried to use them as reserves. The ambitious Teddy, thirsting for action, did an end run around regular troops and went into action. He had ordered a dozen extra pairs of spectacles to take with him, lest poor eyesight, if he broke his glasses, would keep him out of the fight. The "Rough Riders" took San Juan Hill in a spirited action. Roosevelt later wrote about it so glowingly that "Mr. Dooley" said it should have been titled, "Alone in Cuba."

Roosevelt's unconventional attitude spread to his troops. One "Rough Rider," under the impression that he answered only to his own regimental officers, refused to obey an order from a regular army officer. It didn't help that he offered to fight the officer over the issue. He was charged with misconduct, court martialed, and sentenced to a year of hard labor and a dishonorable discharge. However when the regiment landed in Tampa after a short war, and an officer came for the prisoner Roosevelt said, "I pardoned him." The astonished officer said, "You can't do that." The unrepentant answer was, "Well, I did, and he is already mustered out."

The six-weeks war ended just in time, for with the rainy season came mosquitoes, malaria, and yellow fever.

While General Shafter was trying through regular channels to get the army returned home, Roosevelt and other officers sent a "round robin" letter to the press and members of Congress, urging the same. It speeded things up. Some thought T.R. saved the army from a horrible fate.

Roosevelt was elected Vice-President in 1900 and became President when McKinley was shot. He found time for athletic activity and would box with young army officers. One of them delivered a blow which permanently damaged one of Roosevelt's eyes. He kept this a secret for he didn't want to impair the officer's career.

The prime example of his individualism is found in a story he recounted. Two distinguished British army officers came to visit him when he was President. Irritated at their poise and formality he said, "Let's take a walk." Acting as though they were in the presence of a king, they could not refuse or ask to change clothes first. Off they went, through fields and over fences; the Britishers maintaining perfect manners. T.R. felt that "they were beating me at my own game", so he headed for a duck pond, waded in up to his waist while they followed, conversing as if all were normal. Through the pond they went and arrived back at the White House, dripping wet. There they made formal bows and, "like three courtly rats" bade one another "good-bye."

Roosevelt built a strong reputation as a "trustbuster" and was rated by some historians as a "near great" president.

Fuller, Edmund, *Thesaurus of Anecdotes*, New York, Crown Publishers, 1942.
Millis, Walter, *The Martial Spirit*, Boston, Houghton, Miflin Co., 1931.
Steffens, Lincoln, *The Autobiography of Lincoln Steffens*, New York, Harcourt, Brace and Co, 1931.

NOTE: The sinking of the Battleship *Maine* was considered by many to be the immediate cause of the Spanish-American War. A Spanish Commission found it caused by an internal explosion and a U. S. Naval Board of Inquiry held that the explosion was caused by a "submarine mine." Admiral Rickover did a study in 1976 and gave strong evidence that spontaneous combustion in a coal bin next to the powder magazine caused the explosion which sank the ship. The sinking of the *Maine* was not the only reason America went to war with Spain, but it was the immediate cause.

Selling the Basket

A Scottish immigrant boy, Andrew Carnegie, worked hard and saved his money. As a young man he went into the steel manufacturing business in the late 1800s. It was a propitious time as railroads were expanding rapidly and there was a great demand for steel rails. The recently discovered Bessemer process for transforming iron into steel was fundamental to production.

Carnegie built a steel manufacturing empire and became extremely wealthy. He had a formula for success—"Put all your eggs in one basket and watch the basket." By 1901 Carnegie was ready to rid himself of the responsibilities of management and spend more time at his beloved home away from home, "Skibo Castle," in Scotland.

Meantime J.P. Morgan was planning to form a super corporation, U.S. Steel, and he needed the Carnegie interests and others, as the central part of the structure. When the deal came together, U.S. Steel was capitalized at $1.4 billion, the first of its kind. Charles Schwab was the intermediary between the two "masters of capital" and agreement was quickly made to sell the Carnegie Steel Corporation for $400 million. Carnegie took a lead pencil and a sheet of notebook paper and wrote out the terms. Carnegie said, "That's what I will sell for." Morgan replied, "I accept." There was no haggling or debate. The greatest commercial transaction in history was made in this simple manner.

Then Morgan got busy with negotiations with other interests and plans for the new corporation. Suddenly he realized that he had no legal papers or contract, only a gentleman's agreement. He called in his counsel and Carnegie's lawyer, and told them he had organized U.S. Steel on the strength of the oral agreement and did not have a scratch of a pen to protect him, legally. He said, "Go up the street as fast as you can and get me something."

One of the lawyers later said that they went to Carnegie's house and found him in a small room, off the library, dealing with begging letters. Assistants were bringing them in by the bushel. People were asking for everything imaginable including wooden legs. Incidentally, Carnegie was a "soft touch" for an organ request. He loved this musical instrument. The lawyers dictated a contract, with a few interruptions from Carnegie, and it was quickly signed. U.S. Steel, the first billion dollar corporation, was made legal. Carnegie took part of his pay in bonds, refusing stock, as he did not want any responsibility in management.

A year or so later Carnegie was crossing the Atlantic and found J. Pierpont Morgan on the same ship. In conversation, Carnegie mentioned that he had made a mistake in the sale. He said, "I should have asked a hundred million dollars more." Morgan's answer, accompanied by a grin, was, "You would have gotten it if you had."

Someone observed that part of U.S. Steel was formed with "watered stock," that is, there was not enough substance to merit the $1.4 billion which was the level at which it was incorporated. However, U.S. Steel grew so rapidly and successfully that this deficiency was soon corrected.

Hendrick, Burton Jr., *The Life of Andrew Carnegie*, Garden City: Doubleday, Doran and Co., 1932.

Two Georgians

Fishbait Miller

I was in a meeting, years ago, with "Fishbait" Miller, legendary "Doorkeeper" of the House of Representatives. To my surprise I found that this official supervises a staff of 370, in 9 departments. They deal with pages, lobbyists, barber shops, snack bars, custodians, printing, mailing, and the like. They would reproduce and distribute a bill by the next day, even if it was 300 pages long.

When Queen Elizabeth and Prince Phillip visited Congress, he greeted them with, "Howdy Ma'am" and "Howdy Sir." Good manners in Georgia, this greeting was not deemed appropriate for royalty. After this he was sent to diplomatic classes to learn protocol. He would be given a 3x5 card with instructions on what to say. For the Shah of Iran, he would say, "Your Imperial Majesty" and bow from the waist, a difficult feat for a boy from rural Georgia.

Doorkeepers announce honored guests with a bellow heard all over the chamber.

He told of President Ford and Queen Elizabeth standing up to dance in the East Room. The band struck up the tune "The Lady Is a Tramp."

Cultural Stew

Andrew Young has observed that as a melting pot of races and cultures, the United States has been viewed by some as a society resembling a sort of soup without identifiable ingredients. This is neither the way it is nor the way it should be, he says. Rather, the peoples of America make a sort of stew, more desirable than soup. In a good stew the carrot is different from the potato, the meat retains its solid, rich form, and the peas are distinctive, retaining their original color. He meant, of course, that racial and cultural groups could retain their distinctiveness and integrity, yet be blended together in a harmonious whole. [1]

This is reminiscent of Booker T. Washington's favorite illustration of races being separate as the fingers on a hand, yet united to form a hand, complete only when the fingers work together. This was as far as he could go at that time.

[1] In a speech at DeKalb College on May 21, 1971.

Churchill—Master of the English Language

Winston Churchill had a way with words. In his twenties, he was elected to Parliament and made his maiden speech. It was well received. A news reporter wrote an article about it and asked Churchill to review it. At one point the writer had reported "applause" over something the young M.P. said. Churchill marked this out and wrote in the margin, "sustained and thunderous applause." No shrinking violet, he. By this time Churchill had been involved in three wars on three Continents.

The House of Commons allows hoots and catcalls for speakers, even for the Prime Minister, but forbids one M.P. from calling another a liar. Churchill got around this by stating that a colleague was guilty of a "terminological inexactitude." At another time he referred to a political opponent as "a sheep in sheep's clothing." In another speech he spoke of an M.P. leaving the nationalist government to go over to the Labour Party. He made the comment "That it was the first time that he had ever heard of a rat swimming toward a sinking ship."[1]

Churchill made many speeches as Prime Minister. Some are remembered for powerful phrases within them such as "Blood, sweat, toil, and tears" and later, "An iron curtain has descended over Europe."

Winston Churchill was seated near Lady Astor at a dinner. Throughout the evening "He was sharply reproached by Lady Astor for virtually all his political views." Finally the sharp-tongued lady said, "Mr. Churchill, if I were your wife, I should flavor your coffee with arsenic." This was a mistake, as he replied, "And were I your husband, madam, I should drink it."[2]

Historians tended to think this anecdote apocryphal but John Emmett Hughes asserted that Churchill told him the story.

Churchill was a prolific writer, producing over a few years, a six-volume history of World War II and a four-volume history of the English-speaking people. He had a lot of help from secretaries and assistants. Some of them took a dim view of his penchant for ending a sentence with a preposition, if it sounded better. They zealously changed them, which irritated the author. He sent a memo which settled the matter; "This nonsense is arrant pedantry up with which I will not put." His biographer, Taylor, does not include this story when describing the work of Churchill's literary assistants, so I rely on oral history.[3]

[1] Taylor, Robert Lewis, *Winston Churchill*, Garden City, N. Y., Doubleday and Company, Inc. 1952.
[2] Hughes, Emmett John, "Winston Churchill: the Sound of a Man's Voice," *Newsweek*, February 8, 1965.
[3] Various news reports and lectures by professors in graduate school.

Barefoot Johnson and Son

"Barefoot" Johnson also known as "Acrefoot" Johnson, carried the mail from Ft. Meade to Ft. Myers, Florida in the late 1800s. This was a distance of about 80 miles and he made two round trips a week.

This legendary postman, known for his size (6 feet 7 inches), strength, and preference to go barefoot, was one of the colorful characters of the South Florida frontier.

He had a unique way for making some extra money, a sort of taxi service. He would transport a person on his back for ten cents a mile. He rigged a sort of lawn chair, strapped it on his back and let the traveler ride in comfort. Government officials heard of this and with an understandable attitude, put a stop to this personal service.

Johnson was once attacked by three Indians. The fracas started when an Indian jumped out of a tree, onto his back. The last Seminole War was going on and Johnson was caught up in it. He fought them off, throwing one into a nearby creek. Another hazard was that of wild hogs, which would attack only if a herd of them were present. Vern Gaddis, the "flying fisherman," later wrote of being chased up a tree by these pugnacious pigs and he remained there until he was rescued.

The colorful Johnson family tradition was carried on by his son, Guy, "Rattlesnake" Johnson. This member of the family had a well earned nickname, for he caught and bagged more rattlesnakes in DeSoto County, famous for its plethora of these reptiles, than anyone else. During the depression when times were hard and money scarce, Johnson made extra cash by hunting frogs, rattlesnakes, and alligators. He acquired a nationwide reputation and sold snakes to museums and zoos all over the country. Later, men would catch rattlesnakes by putting gasoline down gopher holes, a favorite hiding place for these reptiles. They can't stand the smell and come to the fresh air where they are captured.

Once Guy was bitten by a rattler and gave himself first-aid before going to a local hospital.

He used a snare to catch snakes but occasionally caught them with his bare hands. We are talking about large snakes. I saw a picture of Johnson holding a rattler which appeared to be about six feet long. He caught 294 during the first half of 1932.

George K. End's rattlesnake canning factory in Arcadia agreed to buy all the snakes he could provide. This unique enterprise later moved to Tampa, Florida. As far as I know it has ceased to exist. Perhaps you and I are to blame. How much canned rattlesnake meat have we purchased?

The largely rural area around Arcadia, Florida, with its thousands of acres of palmettos is still a haven for rattlesnakes. Hunters and cattle growers are well aware of the dangers. I met a man named Twiss from Arcadia in the 1960s. He had invented plastic leggings that slipped over the legs below the knees called "Twisters." This provided major protection, for snakes don't usually strike above the knees.

The canning factory is no more, and "Rattlesnake" Johnson has passed off the scene but rattlesnakes remain in DeSoto County, lots of them.

Sources: An article in *Argosy* Magazine, conversations with my brother Gene Adams, who had a fondness for Florida history, and discussions with Howard Melton, historian of DeSoto County. The information about Rattlesnake Johnson came from Howard Melton and his book, *Footprints and Landmarks*, Arcadia and DeSoto County, Florida, 2002. I also talked with "Barefoot" Johnson's grandson, in January, 2005.

Historical Snapshots—20th Century

Frugal Ford

Henry Ford was an ingenious and frugal man. In the early days of his automobile manufacturing business, he contracted with a company to supply automobile parts. The supplier had to meet rigid specifications as to the oak boxes they were shipped in. The wood had to be of high quality, have an exact thickness and the lid had to have holes of a certain size and placement. When the Ford factory used the contents they took the box apart and used the boards. The lid became the floor board of the next new Model-T automobile.[1]

Ford made the assembly line method of manufacturing famous for its economy. Thus he was able to pay top wages ($5 a day), a scale that held the union at bay. He delivered more than they could promise. The retail price for a Model-T dipped below $500.

The number of cars produced was impressive. The 20 millionth Ford (a Model-A), toured the country coming to my school in Brewton, Alabama in 1931.

MacArthur Honored

General Douglas MacArthur fought a brilliant campaign to free the Philippines from cruel Japanese domination in World War II. As the territory was taken and the people set free he would turn it over to the civil authorities. A grateful nation heaped honors on him, one of which was an action of the Philippine Congress that his name be carried in perpetuity on the company rolls of the Philippine Army and at parade roll calls, when his name is called, the senior non-commissioned officer shall answer, "Present in spirit" and during the lifetime of the General he was to be accredited with a guard of honor composed of twelve men of the Philippine Army.[2]

Politics in Action

Adults act in strange and even silly ways during campaigns and in political conventions. Behavior is even more outlandish than the costumes the delegates wear and the signs they bear.

Events don't always work out as planned for these occasions. At one political convention, white doves (or pigeons) were to be released at a high point of excitement. The air-conditioning was not working properly, and the dispirited doves overlong in the cage, refused to fly. The high point became the low point.[1]

In the campaign of 1840, W. H. Harrison was called, as an insult, the "Log Cabin Candidate." He seized upon the term as benefit and used it all the way to victory. Great numbers of voters had lived in log cabins or admired those who did. Harrison lived in a log cabin, sort of. He built a magnificent house around a log cabin, which became his library, the nicest in the West.

112

At some political conventions the band plays an appropriate song as the delegates come in and are seated. One director did not remember his history, for as the Georgia delegation entered, the band struck up "Sherman's March through Georgia." Southerners don't like to think about this.

Sheared on One Side

Secretary of State under Franklin D. Roosevelt, Cordell Hull was the spokesman for the "Good Neighbor Policy" in relation to the Latin American republics. In the finest tradition of diplomats, he was extremely cautious in his statements, striving for accuracy in all details. One day, traveling on a train, his associate pointed to a flock of sheep grazing in a field nearby. Then he said, "Look, those sheep have just been sheared." Looking carefully at the flock, Hull responded, "Sheared on this side, anyway."[3]

Evaluating Faculty

In the history of higher education much has been said about student evaluation of college faculty. Rating of teachers by students dates back to the medieval period. Many times it turned into harassment. An unpopular professor at Dartmouth College, for example, was "rated" by "horning," that is, by students blowing tin horns under his window, as late as 1896.

One unpopular instructor was selected to receive a noisy demonstration one evening. He sat in his office in Thornton Hall as a mob of students, mostly sophomores, gathered outside. They brought with them all kinds of noise-making equipment and made the night hideous with their clamor. The teacher could be seen sitting serenely at his desk and paying no attention to the noise. Angered, they turned up the volume. Snowballs began to fly and then the students began to throw lumps of coal. The windows were shattered.[4]

In the late 1800s faculty members lived on the college campus. Boisterous harassing was common and frequent enough that one person said salaries were quoted with the phrase added "With coal thrown in."

The story is told of the Arkansas legislature discussing voting funds for a state university. A question arose over faculty teaching load and a twelve-hour load was reported. One legislator said, "That is a long day but it's light work."

[1] Guide at the Ford Museum.
[2] Douglas MacArthur, *Reminiscences*, page 307.
[3] Fuller, Edmund, *Thesaurus of Anecdotes*, New York, Crown Publishers, 1942.
[4] Courley, W. H., *Improving College and University Teaching*, November 1953.

Sergeant York

Ask older Americans who was the greatest hero in World War I and the overwhelming number would likely say "Sergeant Alvin York." Why would people look past General "Black Jack" Pershing, young General Douglas MacArthur and other winners of the Congressional Medal of Honor and name Alvin C. York? Perhaps it is because he whipped a whole battalion in a fair fight, killed 25 Germans, and captured 132 others, thereby saving hundreds of American lives.

His is a fascinating story. He was born in northern Tennessee in the valley of the Three Forks of the Wolf, so named by Coonrod Pike, one of the "long hunters." In 1771 Pike returned to Virginia, married, and brought his bride to this isolated valley. Here he raised a large family and became a prosperous landowner. In the early 1900s, William York, Alvin's father, was living in the valley, having been born in the cabin of the "long hunter." He did his blacksmith work in the cave where Coonrod Pike first lived. Incidentally, caves in this part of the country are set in limestone bluffs, are often wider in the mouth than in the interior, and are called "rock houses." There is a large one next to the highway between Jamestown and Pall Mall.

William York was a mighty hunter, a strong and fearless man, but he died of typhoid fever. He left a wife and eleven children, most of them red-headed, in a one-room cabin, fifty miles from the nearest railroad. Alvin was the third child, in this Scotch-Irish family.

Alvin York's mother was a remarkable woman, as a widow raising eleven children on a hillside farm. Tom Skeyhill interviewed her and asked why Alvin was the biggest of them all. She answered, "When he was young, I whipped him that much that I kept his skin loose so he had plenty of room to fill out."[1]

When her son returned from France as a hero "Mother York" consented to attend a reception in his honor in Nashville, but she refused to wear "city clothes." She wore linsey dress, bonnet, and shawl, as she did in the mountains and was a hit with the crowd.

Lacking in formal education, Alvin C. York lived in the forest, learned about nature, became a mighty hunter, the best shot in the community, and developed into a strong, self-reliant man. There is no evading the fact that Alvin York went through a wild period as a young man, drinking, fighting, and gambling. But he made a great change in 1915, when be was converted, "saved," as he put it, by the influence of an evangelist and his loving, patient mother. He became a song leader and Sunday School teacher in the little valley church. The community took note of the profound change in his life.

Then war came and Alvin received a notice to register for the draft. A pacifist at heart, he wrote on the bottom of the registration card "I don't want to fight." As a member of "The Church of Christ in Christian Union" he was a conscientious objector. He appealed his case all the way to President Wilson, but he was drafted anyway. He reported to Camp Gordon, Georgia and was assigned as a private to the 82nd Division. Here he impressed his captain with devotion to duty and skill with a rifle. This officer referred the problem of York's conscientious objections to fighting, to Major Burton, who had experience in dealing with the issue and had studied the Bible in connection with it.

In the remarkable interview, the Captain witnessing it, the Major and the private quoted Scripture back and forth dealing with the question of killing in time of war. York later said that he was glad that the Major "knowed such a mighty lot about the Bible." Then the Major, convinced of York's sincerity, gave him two weeks leave to go home and think it over. Here he wrestled with the problem, at one time praying for thirty-six hours on the mountainside. He broke through to a clear decision and told his mother he was going to war "with the sword of the Lord and of Gideon." He rejoined his outfit and went to France, arriving in May, 1918. The action for which he is best remembered came in the fall of that year.

General Pershing's army launched the Meuse-Argonne offensive from September 26 to November 11,

1918. Several million men were involved. His objective was to cut the German railroad lines supplying the western front.

It was a terrible battle, lasting forty-seven days, using 1.2 million American troops. The heaviest fighting was in the Argonne Forest. Ten thousand of the American soldiers were killed or wounded. Progress was slow because of German machine guns, firing from concealed positions.

Early on the morning of October 8, York's 2nd Battalion, 328th Infantry, attacked the Germans from Hill 223 in the Argonne Forest. Company G, commanded by Captain Danforth, advanced against the Germans through a small valley. Withering machine gun fire poured into the doughboys from the front, from a steep hill to the right, and from a wooded hill to the left. Losses were heavy, but then the firing slackened from the left. Corporal Alvin York had arrived.

The 1st Platoon, commanded by Sergeant Parsons after Lt. Stewart was killed, was stopped, its front line mowed down. The machine guns, entrenched in the ridges and brush, had to be silenced or the advance would fail. He gave an order that seemed like certain death. York's squad circled behind the German position, advanced through the thick brush and came upon a clearing where there was a machine gun regiment headquarters with about a hundred men gathered there. On the steep hill nearby, machine guns firing in the other direction were reversed and began firing down into the clearing at York and his men. The remaining soldiers found cover but Corporal York stood in the open, firing his rifle until ammunition was gone and then using his pistol. The Germans in the clearing surrendered, after several were shot, and then an officer called on the machine gunners to cease fire and surrender. All at once York had about 100 prisoners and it was a long way back to the command post. When a German officer asked how many men he had York replied, "I've got a plenty."

Surrender was not total. A German officer and six soldiers caught on that they had only one man to deal with, jumped from their nearby gun pit and rushed him with naked steel. York drew his pistol and put on an amazing demonstration of accurate shooting. He dropped the last man first, then the 6th and so on, until all seven were lined out in a neat row. When asked later, he explained that had he shot the leading one first the others would have scattered.

York lined the Germans up in two columns, with two soldiers on the left, two on the right, and two in the rear, with bayonets. He was in the lead, a pistol in each hand, a major in front and a German officer on either side. He marched them through the German lines and came under heavy fire. He put a pistol in the major's ribs, ordered him to blow his whistle signaling surrender and said, "Blow that thar whistle again, and blow it right smart." This was done and about 30 more prisoners were added. He marched them across no man's land and turned them over to the intelligence officer, Lt. Woods, who counted 132. In answer to his question, "Good Lord, have you captured the whole German army?" Corporal York replied, "I've got a tolable few." He had taken 35 machine guns and was credited with killing 25 enemy soldiers. (Bailey says it was 20.)[2]

York's exploit was so incredible that the army couldn't believe it. Investigation after investigation was launched and reports were taken from Captain Danforth, Sergeant Parsons and others. They all verified that Alvin

C. York, with little assistance, attacked a German machine gun regiment, killed 25 Germans and captured 132 others. He became a sergeant and an American hero.

[1] Skeyhill, Tom, *Sergeant York*, *Last of the Long Hunters*, Larry Harrison, St. John, Indiana, Knickerbocker (no publication date listed).
[2] Bailey, Thomas A., Kennedy, David A., *The American Pageant*, ninth edition, Lexington, Mass. 1991.

New Deal Projects, Wild and Worthwhile

The Great Depression stalked the land in the early 1930s. Unemployment was high, wages were low, and millions of people were on the verge of starvation. Living was precarious on our south Alabama farm, but we did have the ability to produce food—corn, cane (we made our own syrup), sweet potatoes, and field peas. Women canned fruit and vegetables and pork was cured in the smokehouse.

President Roosevelt launched a flurry of "New Deal" projects after he took office in 1933. One of these was provided by the Agricultural Adjustment Act (A.A.A.) which paid farmers not to raise crops, and to plow under some already growing. Farmers were also paid to slaughter pigs and bury them. Inspectors checked to see that it was done. Some wag wrote a poem for a farm magazine, and, after all these years I remember a few lines:

> Little Boy Blue
> Come blow your horn,
> A government agent
> Is counting your corn.
>
> Another is lecturing
> The old red sow,

On how many pigs
She can have, and how.

The hired man quit
Cause the work didn't please,
And got a job
Trimming government trees.

Aunt Mame is in Washington
Dragging down pay
From the P.D.Q.
Or the A.A.A.

Mercifully, that's all I remember. I do believe that truth lurks within this doggerel.

Then there was P.W.A. and W.P.A. designed to put men to work and get money into people's pockets as quickly as possible. There was a lot of wasted effort and W.P.A. was said to stand for "We piddle around."

Dr. Batten, Vanderbilt professor, told our class about his observation of mismanagement. There was a small, grassy triangle where 21st Avenue intersects Division Street, near Vanderbilt Divinity School. This narrow triangle is about forty feet long and twenty feet wide at its widest point. He watched from his office window as a truckload of men arrived, along with wheelbarrows, picks and shovels. They were to dig up and seed this tiny piece of public real estate. There was standing room only. My kindly old professor, with a twinkle in his eye, said, "If all those men had started swinging their picks at once, Vanderbilt Hospital could not have taken care of the casualties."

However there were public works of lasting value. Federal funds were used to build courthouses, bridges, and buildings in state parks. Solid work was done, using native stone and many of these works of art are still in use seventy-five years later.

One of the finest enduring accomplishments of the "New Deal" was the creative project of building homesteads on the Cumberland Plateau, four miles south of Crossville, Tennessee. The Government agency, The Federal Division of Subsistence Homesteads, bought 10,000 acres of land, made tracts available to poor people who qualified, and helped 252 families buy land and build houses. Tracts were available, up to ninety acres, but I was told, when visiting this settlement, that twenty acres was a typical size.

By the middle of 1934 construction was underway on roads, houses, and barns. Over 1,000 families applied and were fully screened for "character, honesty, willingness to work, and willingness to cooperate, and willingness to improve the farm." Selected participants worked for fifty cents an hour, one third of which was withheld for down payment. The homesteader helped build the house under supervision of skilled construction people. The buyer had thirty years to pay off a mortgage that averaged about $2,000.

The 252 houses were built using several different plans but as you drive through the countryside viewing these houses, there seems to be a common design feature. Perhaps it is the beautiful Crab Orchard stone (now terribly expensive) from nearby quarries. The houses I saw were all two stories high. Wells were drilled for water and every house was wired for electricity, not usually available in rural America at that time.

At a central spot an octagonal edifice was built and rising above it, a 50,000 gallon water tower. Today the tower houses the Cumberland Homesteads Museum, open to the public, March to November.

These beautiful houses, scattered for miles across the countryside, remind us of one of the enduring success stories of the "New Deal."

Interview with people in the community.
An article by Leon Allgood, "TDOT Plan Would Remove Historic Land," *The Tennessean,* 4/25/05.

The Kingfish

Huey Long was one of the most colorful politicians the United States has ever produced. He had all the characteristics of a political boss and dominated Louisiana politics in the 1920s and 1930s as governor. He had a loyal following who liked his flamboyant, benign, dictatorship style.

An ardent football fan, he offered to take the entire student body of L.S.U., 5,000 strong, on a train to Nashville for a game with Vanderbilt University.

"Red" Heard told the story of the Governor dropping in to his L.S.U. athletic office to inquire about an upcoming game and how the attendance would be. He heard that the numbers would be down because the Ringling Circus was scheduled to be in town that weekend.

Long asked to use the phone and placed a call to John Ringling in Sarasota, Florida. The Governor joked around a little and then asked that the Circus cancel its trip to Baton Rouge that week-end and re-schedule. A lengthy response came from the owner, telling of contracts let, plans made, and the impossibility of cancelling on short notice. Long brushed that aside and proceeded to instruct Ringling on the Louisiana Stock-Dip Law. This statute required livestock entering the state to be dipped in tanks of chemicals to kill ticks. Then came the punch line, "Sir, did you ever try to dip a tiger?" The conversation ended with the Kingfish thanking the Circus owner for agreeing to cancel the trip to Baton Rouge.[1]

Events took an unusual turn in 1930 when Governor Long was elected to the U.S. Senate. It was not clear as to when he ceased to be Governor and became a Senator. In 1931 and 1932 a momentous struggle took place in which there were two contenders for the office of Governor and Lieutenant-Governor of the state. Long did not like Paul Cyr, the Lieutenant-Governor, and made every effort to keep him from assuming the Governor's office. He asserted that he would still be Governor until sworn in as U. S. Senator.

In October, 1931, Cyr attempted to take possession of the Governor's office and was sworn in. Long knew that the issue of his retention of the office until he became a Senator would later be solved by the Legislature. However, he was convinced that the Lieutenant-Governor's office was now vacant and that Cyr was neither Governor nor Lieutenant-Governor. Therefore he arranged for the President Pro Tem of the Senate, Alvin G. King, constitutionally qualified, to become Lieutenant-Governor. A dispute over who should draw the salary for the office was settled when the Attorney General ruled that it go to King.

King was sworn in as Governor of Louisiana in January, 1932, and Huey Long went to Washington to be a member of the U.S. Senate. Cyr wouldn't give up. He found a deputy clerk of court who swore him in as Governor. Long sent word back that an inquiry should be made into Cyr's sanity. Cyr declared his seat of government to be a room in the Heidelberg Hotel. From this obscure position he issued proclamations against the King government. He was ejected from the hotel but issued one final diatribe about the "high-handed treason" of King and Long. Then he just faded away.[2]

Long did not fade away. He went on to make lengthy speeches, one listed in the Congressional Record, giving details on how to cook turnip greens Louisiana style. A black, iron pot was required and smoked pork included as seasoning. He was assassinated at the Louisiana State Capital in 1935.

The common man loved Huey Long and what he promised them in Louisiana. An uncle of mine lived there during the Huey Long years and had nothing but praise for him.

[1] The story told by "Red" Heard about dipping the tiger was recounted by McGill, Ralph, *Nashville Tennessean*, June 9, 1959.
[2] The struggle for the governorship is found in Harris, Thomas G., *The Kingfish*, New Orleans, Pelican Publishing Company, 1938.

Humor in Wartime

The history of wars in the Twentieth Century can be traced by what soldiers and sailors think is funny. From World War I, where the action was on the "front," comes the story of the private who ran for the rear, when the battle was at its worst. He was halted by a high-ranking officer who demanded that he give an account of himself. He reprimanded the private severely, saying, "I am your commanding general." The frightened soldier said, "I knew I ran a long way, but I didn't know I had come that far back to where the generals were."

Another concerned the chaplain who held a prayer meeting the night before a big battle. He called on a private to lead in prayer. This young soldier included in his petition "And tomorrow in the battle, Oh Lord, let the bullets be divided, like the pay, mostly among the officers."[1]

A new, very young, second lieutenant reported for duty. At the first muster of his platoon, a solo voice from the rear rank was heard to say, "And a little child shall lead them." He made no response, but posted an order on the bulletin board which read, "First platoon will fall out at daybreak for a three mile march, with full field packs. And a little child will lead them—on a great, big horse."

In World War II, a soldier, from deep within the country, newly drafted, was assigned sentry duty. He was drilled over and over to say "Halt! Who goes there? Give the counter-sign." However, his first customer was the base commander, whose car stopped, flag with stars, flapping. The over-awed young soldier yelled "Halt! Look who's heah!"

During the Vietnam war, the draft was on, and many young men tried to evade military service. However, one man rushed into a draft board office, flung his shirt open, and cried, "Stamp me 1-A. Sign me up! Let me at that Charlie Cong! I love those steaming jungles." The doctor said, "Man, you're crazy." The answer was, "Write it down, Doctor, write it down!"

Deriding the enemy was a favorite brand of humor in World War II. When the British armored force routed the Italian tanks in North Africa, someone observed "The Italians are equipping their tanks with rear-view mirrors so as to see the enemy approaching."

Certain events are more humorous than wartime jokes. Walter Lord, writing about the Pearl Harbor attack, told of two young sailors leaping from a damaged battleship to swim to shore. They were making good progress, when from behind them, they heard a cry for help. An old chief petty officer, yelled "Help me; I can't swim." They heard thrashing sounds in the water, and he passed them, yelling "Help me; I can't swim." He beat them to shore![2]

During war, military people engage in humor, often crude, to ease tension and break the monotony.

[1] Regarding the jokes, who knows who to credit? Humor is in the public domain.
[2] The story about Pearl Harbor is found in Walter Lord, *Day of Infamy*, New York, Bantam Books, 1991.

Food for Soldiers and Sailors

In wartime food is very important for health and morale. Soldiers in the field in World War II existed on K rations and griped while they ate them. It wasn't much better in the Navy, especially in small ships. The crew members in my ship once collected money and bought bread in a local bakery in Suva, Fiji.

In 1944–45 our sub-chaser worked with mine sweepers. They would cut the mine cables and we would sink them, or blow them up with armor piercing ammunition. When one of the 500 pound monsters blew up, the explosion would stun or kill fish for a hundred yards around. We had all the fresh grouper we could eat, and once supplied the shore-based Navy at the section base, with fresh fish. Strangely, many of the men aboard my ship refused to eat fish, typical of an age-old prejudice among sailors.

When we were engaged in anti-sub patrol, at four knots, ideal trolling speed, some of the men would sit in the ship's boat, hoisted at the stern, and let out the fishing lines. The biggest catch I remember was a six-foot long Lihue Tuna. How to get the fish aboard was a problem, quickly solved. Two men held my ankles while I hung head down, six feet, and secured a line around the tuna's forked tail. Then they hoisted man and fish aboard. It made excellent steaks.

One final word about food. Ships in the South Pacific, under reverse lend-lease, could get wonderful jams and jellies from Australia and New Zealand. I have seen my Skipper sit down at the table, take one look at the food, and then make a meal of bread, butter, and strawberry preserves.

Whatever the food, soldiers and sailors complained and a favorite word for the cook was "belly robber."

As Executive Officer of the ship, I would occasionally go ashore, borrow a jeep and look for fruit. In the New Hebrides Islands, I have found avocadoes, on abandoned native farms, and groves of mango trees. Once I found a stalk of bananas, ready to pick, but a wild boar was standing next to the tree. He didn't move; I did. I was packing a 45-caliber automatic but it was not too accurate, fifty feet away. Once I checked out a weapons carrier, loaded several sailors in it, and went into the mountains of New Caledonia to hunt deer, while the ship was in for repair. We brought back a big buck, but most of the men wouldn't eat venison.

Source: Personal experience and observations.

Unsung Heroes

To render service is a wonderful thing. To do so with no hope of reward, not even recognition of the noble deed, is heroic. It was World War II in the Southwest Pacific. My ship was Sub-chaser 1268, one of the little ships, part of the "Donald Duck Navy," as some would say. It was 110 feet long and 18 feet in the beam. Twenty-seven officers and men served on board, in quarters well-nigh as cramped as those in a submarine.

We had little room for storage, with refrigerator/freezer space being scant indeed. That mattered little during those months when fresh meat and vegetables were unavailable. Like other sub-chaser and minesweeper crews, we ate an _awful_ lot of Spam and Vienna sausage. Underscore awful! Then in Noumea, New Caledonia, when I took a work party to the naval supply to draw rations, I was told, "Fresh vegetables are available!" I couldn't believe it. We requisitioned crates of cabbage, green corn, and even watermelons. What a feast and what a blessing! Word had it (never underestimate the validity of scuttle-butt) that these vegetables were provided by a small Naval group on one of the New Hebrides Islands, north of us. The war had shifted to the Philippines, where MacArthur had just "returned." There was little for these sailors to do and you know the problem with idle hands.

The Lieutenant in charge, with a farm background no doubt, put his men to work raising vegetables. The soil was rich, the crop abundant, and they rendered special service to the Navy for hundreds of miles around. Where he got tools and seeds I'll never know. Perhaps I should have asked Jim Michener who was writing _Tales of the South Pacific_ at Espiritu Santo, nearby.

After months of Spam and beans, to sit down to fresh cabbage and cornbread was a treat. To an unsung and unknown Naval officer and his men, sixty years later, I send a heartfelt "Thank you."

Source: Personal experience.

Note: ABC sent Diane Sawyer back to Espiritu Santo with Michener, fifty years later, to commemorate his epic writing. The T.V. camera showed them standing on the slope, near where a small wharf used to be, conducting the interview. I wrote Diane that this was the spot where her illustrious father, Lt. Erbon ("Tom") Sawyer, took command of Sub-chaser 1268, on which I served. She and her mother appreciated learning this. Sawyer, a leading judge in Louisville, Kentucky, had been killed in an auto accident a few years before.

Life on the Old Farm

Those of us with rural origins are often prone to think of what life was like on the old farm. This leads to nostalgic rush of memories about those earlier days in all seasons. I remember as vividly as yesterday—the sounds, the smells, the tastes, and the scenes of a bygone era.

The sounds echoing across the years . . .

The regular squeaking of the windlass as a bucket of water is winched upward from deep within the well.

The faint but melodious whisper of a ripe watermelon cracking open along the track of the case knife inserted in its cool, green flank.

The clucking murmur from the hen-roost as the door is carefully closed at deep dusk.

The distant sounds of a neighbor's frequent exhortations to the recalcitrant mule he is plowing in the young corn.

129

The drumming of falling pecans as slender branches are shaken by a small boy perched high in the tree.

The ringing yodel of the hound of uncertain origin, sounding on a clear night, in anxious pursuit of a possum.

The tiny explosions of bubbles of ribbon cane syrup boiling upward in the steaming vat at syrup-making time late in November.

The sound of an axe wielded on a frosty morning, punctuated by the whirring of an errant chip of fat pine.

The smells of field and wood and home . . .

The pungent odor of dry pine needles kicked into glistening heaps by boys' feet sliding down the carpeted slope.

The dusty smell of sun-washed hay into which one plunges from the rafters of the hay mow.

The raw incense of turpentine rising from a new-cut pine and mingled with the smell of kerosene sprinkled on the blade of the cross-cut saw.

The mingled flavor of oak and pine that rises from the big box by the kitchen stove as a "turn" of stove wood is dumped therein.

The smell of homemade sausage, redolent with sage, sizzling in the skillet.

The fragrant breath of hickory smoke curling from the eaves of the smokehouse, bearing a whiff of hams and shoulders curing within.

The tastes, reminiscent of an early day . . .

A cold biscuit, permeated with syrup from a hole punched in its flaky side, and, after a three-mile walk home from school, barely easing the appetite until suppertime.

The tangy sweetness of purple muscadines, fresh-fallen from the vine in the tall black-gum tree.

The sandstone flavor of cold well water, gulped from a gourd dipper plunged into a brimming bucket.

Crusty, crackling break lifted in large bites from tall goblets of creamy, sweet milk at supper time in the big dining room.

The tender saltiness of fresh green peanuts boiled in the large black pot.

The puckering bite of a plump orange persimmon, picked just before the first frost falls.

The scenes revealed again by the eye of memory . . .

The sight of waving rows of tasseled corn, marching over the gentle hill between the wider spaced rows of young pecan trees.

The crystal water of the poplar-shaded spring, every detail of its sandy bottom clearly outlined to one lying prone to drink.

The close-up view of the succulent half of a "Stone Mountain" watermelon, tiny red granules of sugary sweetness glistening around the heart.

Heat waves shimmering above the cotton patch on a late July day.

The rushing waters of the leaf-stained creek rippling just beneath the mossy foot-log.

The farmhouse seen from a distance, blue smoke curling skyward, a flight of doves in arrow-swift flight outlined against the sky above.

The sight of the red-berried holly Christmas tree, festooned with long strings of popcorn and the vision of the exciting presents beneath—a book, oranges, red-stick candy, an apple, a small toy, and a cluster of raisins.

The Southern Country Store

The country store in the 1800s and early 1900s was the center of activity for farmers and their families for miles around. Near my home in Antioch, Alabama, ten miles north of the county seat and where two dirt roads crossed, there was a typical country store, owned by a distant cousin, Seth Stewart.

It was like the country stores described by T.D. Clark in his book *Pills, Petticoats and Plows.*[1] It was the only one available within three miles, where there was a similar establishment. The nearest town was ten miles away, and it took all day for the round trip in a two-horse wagon. That didn't leave much time for shopping, and for selling the sweet potatoes, peanuts, or watermelons the farmer brought with him. Thus people in the community were bound to trade at Stewart's store or to one of those described by Clark, for kerosene, patent medicine, groceries, feed, seed, and fertilizer.

And there was the matter of credit. On the seed and fertilizer, giving credit often meant the storekeeper had to wait until the crop was harvested and sold to collect his money. In our community the crop was cotton and the fertilizer was guano. Often groceries, kerosene, and coffee were purchased on credit as well, unless the farm wife brought in eggs or live chickens to barter for these items.

It must be admitted that there was some competition—the "rolling store," though this might be owned by the storekeeper. This was a covered truck with an aisle down the middle and shelves on either side loaded with groceries. At the back was a kerosene drum and crates to receive the chickens taken in barter. The rolling store stopped in front of each farmhouse, honked the horn and waited to swap a pound of coffee for a dozen eggs. Of course, some cash was exchanged. Rolling stores are no more and it would be interesting to know when the last one rolled down the red clay roads of Alabama, Georgia, or Tennessee. The last I heard of was in 1940.

Clark mentions the stores that sold whiskey. He told of one merchant who had trouble preventing theft. Some thirsty and creative miscreant crawled under the floor of the store, bored with an auger, through the floor and the bottom of the barrel, installed a spigot, thus providing himself with a regular supply of 90-proof. The store-keeper put a stop to that. He put the whiskey barrel on rollers and moved it at the end of each day. Then he found a row of auger holes seeking to connect with the barrel.

Groceries selling whiskey were common throughout rural America in the 1800s. Abraham Lincoln worked in a grocery in Illinois which dispensed strong drink. Later in the famous Lincoln-Douglas debates, Douglas taunted Lincoln about this. Lincoln said, "It is true that I stood behind the counter in a grocery and sold whiskey. However I would point out that I left my side of the counter but my opponent has not left his side." The crowed roared, for all knew that Douglas was fond of this adult refreshment.

A country store near a railroad had an advantage in prices and convenience for receiving groceries and other supplies. It wasn't always profitable to the railroad. My political science professor at Vanderbilt University, Dr. Clarence Nixon, told of his father's country store in north Alabama. He remembered the train putting on brakes a quarter of a mile away and stopping near the store long enough to unload one case of sardines. I think he put this story, and others, in a book titled *Possum Trot*, but I never read it.

Country stores have changed. Storekeepers no longer serve as both grocers and bankers, and there is a Wal-Mart within driving distance.

After T.D. Clark, of the University of Kentucky, wrote *Pills, Petticoats and Plows*, he developed interest in another aspect of social history, "decoration day" in southern churches and their adjacent cemeteries. He came to Nashville when I was teaching at Trevecca College to make inquiry about this custom. He had the impression that funeral services were held again and again. I was able to explain that it was a matter of bringing flowers, often on the third Sunday in May, to decorate the graves of relatives. People would stand around and talk, reminisce about the inhabitants of the silent city of the dead, and then go into the church for worship. It was a homecoming event culminating with dinner on the grounds.

Each year, my wife and I return to the little country church, 150 miles away, to join in this memorial event with kinfolks and friends. Thousands of others do the same. Try to get a motel room in Walker County, Alabama on the third or fourth weekend in May and you will see what I mean.[2]

[1] Clark, T. D., *Pills, Petticoats and Plows*, Indianapolis, The Bobbs-Merrill Co., 1944.
[2] Personal observation.

Secret Mission

During World War II the Vichy French government collaborated with Hitler's Germany and was therefore an enemy to the United States and her allies. However there was a chance that French military leaders in North Africa could be swung over to the side of the Allies. The Allied invasion of North Africa, November 8, 1942, was preceded by a "cloak and dagger" mission led by General Mark Clark to try to persuade the French not to oppose the Allies. It would be enough to engage Italian and German armies in North Africa.

The mission had all the elements of a James Bond novel—arriving off the coast at night in a submarine, paddling through the surf in a small boat, guided by a signal light in a seaward window. They even carried a thousand dollars in gold pieces to buy their way out of a tight spot, if need be. They carried civilian clothes in case they needed to become full-fledged spies.

The plan was to meet the French Commander, General Nast, at a secret rendezvous near Algiers, and work out an agreement to avoid the conflict that threatened. On reaching shore, Clark and his associates, carrying their boat and equipment, rushed to the shelter of some olive trees and from there to the isolated villa, the site of the secret meeting. This started at 5:00 A.M. and led to the revolt of the French forces from the Vichy Government.

Then word came that the Arab servants in the villa had informed the police, who were now on their way to raid the place. Frenchmen disappeared in all directions and one of Clark's commandos made his way to the beach to warn the waiting sub. Clark and the rest of the team tumbled through a trap-door, into a wine cellar. They huddled there, pistols in hand, trying for total silence while the police searched overhead. A British commando was seized with a coughing fit, and whispered to the General, "I'm afraid I'll choke!" To this Clark replied "I'm afraid you won't." Then he popped a wad of gum in the soldier's mouth, which solved the problem. Later the commando complained about the lack of flavor in the gum. Clark had to explain that he had already chewed the flavor out of it.

The police left and the daring team made their way through the turbulent breakers, and, in their little canvas boat, paddled back to the waiting submarine. They bore vital information to the allies, namely that there would be no French resistance to the Allied invasion.

The only misfortune was the loss of General Clark's pants in the heavy surf. They washed ashore and were found by the French, who returned them to him, neatly cleaned and pressed. Unfortunately they had shrunk to knee-length shorts in the salt water!

Clark, Mark W., *Calculated Risk*, New York, Harper and Brothers, 1950.

D-Day 1944 and Beyond

The cross-channel invasion of German held Europe was the greatest military operation in history. On June 6, 1944, hundreds of ships, and almost a million allied troops attacked the Norman coast of France, under skies darkened by thousands of airplanes.

The fateful date for the attack was in doubt until the very last. A target date in May had been scrapped and June 4 chosen. High winds, low clouds, and hazardous waves made the attack unfavorable on that day. The Supreme Commander of the Allied Expeditionary Force, General Dwight D. Eisenhower, postponed operation "Overlord" as it was called. Ships and troops, already at sea, were recalled. Southern England was a vast military camp and Eisenhower was in a tent in the midst of the force. After hurricane-like winds hit early on June 5 he went, through the mud, to a conference at naval headquarters. There he and his commanders learned from the meteorologists that there would be, on the following morning, unexpected, good weather and that it would last thirty-six hours. Eisenhower quickly announced the attack for June 6.

Eisenhower had been confronted with pessimism and opposition for months. Churchill had doubts about Overlord and frequently voiced them. However, in his book, *Closing the Ring*, Churchill denied this, saying, "It was not that I was in any way lukewarm about Overlord." The General, a sort of military statesman, would meet the gloomy predictions with optimism and go ahead with the plan. To Churchill's complaint, about thirty-six divisions being used, Eisenhower countered, that there would be another ten from Italy, and forty more divisions from the U.S., when the French ports were open. As late as May 30, Air Marshal Leigh-Mallory was protesting the terrible slaughter that would result from the airborne operation on the Cherbourg Peninsula. He thought the hazards were too great to overcome. Eisenhower shook it off and proceeded with the plan.

A number of people on the Supreme Commander's staff appealed for permission to go with the attacking force in naval ships, as military staff are wont to do. It was easier to say "No" to them than to Winston Churchill, who insisted on joining the expeditionary force. He had been involved in military action in India, Sudan, the Boer War, and World War I and his warrior blood demanded that he take part in this great struggle. Denied permission to go with the military forces he slyly reminded Eisenhower that he could go as part of a ship's company which the General did not control. Eisenhower acknowledged this but pointed out that the danger of his becoming a casualty would add another burden to the General. Then help came from an unexpected quarter. The King sent word that, while he would not interfere with the Prime Minister's decision, he would find it his duty also, to place himself at the head of his troops. Churchill dropped the idea.

The massive assault on the Norman coast was complex and bloody, with 4,000 ships and 8,000 planes involved. Amphibious ships, disgorged men, and vehicles, hundreds of warships fired on German emplacements, and men fought their way across the beach amid a hail of bullets, before working their way up sheer cliffs, defended by Germans in strong emplacements. The beachhead was secured and then expanded providing adequate supply routes by the end of June. The allies took 41,000 prisoners but had 60,771 casualties of whom 8,975 were killed.

After heavy fighting in July the allied armies enveloped the German forces west of the Seine and the eventual defeat of Hitler's forces became a certainty. Then Eisenhower and Churchill had another disagreement, this one over "Dragoon," a landing in the south of France, under General Devers. The Prime Minister finally gave in.

Prime Minister Winston Churchill saw himself as a military strategist as well as one with political insight and favored dealing with post-war Europe while the war to free it was underway. Thus he persuaded the allies to attack the "soft, underbelly of Europe" by way of the campaign in Italy. No doubt he was thinking of England's interests in Greece and other parts of the Mediterranean. The wisdom of this strategy is still in question.

He opposed the thrust from the South of France in 1944, preferring an invasion through the Balkans. He knew that region would be more stable after the war if England, and the U.S. were in control rather than the Russians. Stalin was also aware of post-war politics in a way that FDR. was not.

The inexorable advance of allied forces during the summer and fall of 1944, the "Battle of the Bulge" in mid-winter, and Germany's surrender on May 8, 1945, is a fascinating study!

Eisenhower emerged from the war as a genuine American hero, one on the way to the American presidency.

Eisenhower, Dwight D., *In Review*, Garden City, New York, Doubleday and Company, Inc., 1969.
Churchill, Winston, *Closing The Ring*, New York, Houghton Miflin Co., 1951.

Falls and Survivors

Some amazing stories came out of World War II about dangerous falls and survivors. One sticks in my memory as clearly as when I read it during the war. It was that of a light bomber, an A-20, with a two man crew, on a training flight over Canada, in the deep of winter. For some reason the bomb-bay door flew open and the crew member went back to deal with it. The pilot heard a shout, and looked back to see that the airman had fallen through the opening and was desperately clinging to the steel ridge around the door.

The pilot could not leave the controls so he swung the plane low over an ice-covered lake and headed for a snowbank. He hoped his crew-mate would fall into it but did not learn until later that this happened. The airman went into the snow, which cushioned his fall, and emerged from it to slide across the ice for half a mile. Protected by heavy leather flying gear, he escaped serious injury and was rescued by ice fishermen.

While serving in the Navy in the Pacific, I was told of a Navy pilot, forced to bail out of his plane. His parachute failed to open and he fell 2,000 feet into the ocean. He survived, though with two broken legs. He said he stiffened his body and hit feet first.

My brother's B-24 bomber was shot up over Germany and went down in the North Sea. He and two others, out of a crew of ten, escaped and took to a rubber raft. They had time to transmit "Mayday," and could hear planes searching for them. A break came in the overcast and a plane miraculously appeared in the patch of blue. They were spotted and rescued.

My brother, Gene, also told me about a B-17 so heavily damaged over enemy territory that the plane broke in two near the tail section. The tail-gunner inside rode the fragment, fluttering from side to side like a leaf, to the ground. He stepped out, unscathed, and was taken prisoner.

Another account out of Europe during World War II, was that of a pilot whose chute did not open. He dropped into a large fir tree and fell through it, breaking limb after limb, each of which slowed his descent. He suffered injuries but survived the ordeal.

A similar escape was reported by Oluf Olsen in *Assignment Spy*. His chute partly opened when he dropped into Norway to fight Germans.

General Mark Clark commanded troops in Italy during World War II. This "soft underbelly of Europe," as Winston Churchill euphemistically described it, turned out to be very tough. General Clark liked to check on forward positions of his forces, by plane. In a light L-5 plane, sometimes called a "grasshopper," he and his pilot would fly very low over fields and hedges near the front lines. One day they flew too low and hit a tall flagpole. The plane was impaled on the pole, and started spinning around and around like a child's toy. It worked its way to the ground and the two soldiers stepped out and walked away.[1]

On a much less dramatic note, I took a fall on Subchaser 1268, from the flying bridge to the deck alongside the pilot house. We were painting the ship, an "all hands" operation. As Gunnery Officer, I joined in the fun. I was on a narrow strip of deck, outside the canvas windbreaker that surrounded the bridge, painting the canvas. I leaned back but held the barrel of the signal mortar placed there. It was supposed to be bolted to the deck but it wasn't. I fell about ten feet, barely missing the rocket ready box, with the mortar tumbling after me. It hit the deck beside me, its barrel scraping my back. I got up and sheepishly walked away, hoping no one saw it. My gunner's mates would have had great fun with this free fall. To this day I don't know what happened to the bucket of paint.[2]

[1] Clark, Mark, *Calculated Risk*, New York, Harper and Brothers, 1950.
[2] Various news reports. In the Pacific, most of our news came from Armed Forces Radio. The A-20 accident was covered in a news magazine.

Governor in a Sweat

College registrars have an interesting job and they have been around a long time. In the medieval university the registrar was known as "the right honorable beadle." They guard academic records, control diplomas at graduation, and order academic regalia.

The Registrar at Georgia Southwestern College (now University) told me an interesting story about graduation in his institution, years ago.

Governor Lester Maddox, a colorful and controversial politician, was the commencement speaker. The President called the Registrar into his office, gave instructions for ordering cap and gown for the Governor and said, "Order the heaviest wool robe that can be found." He had tried in vain to get the gym air-conditioned and he had a plan.

Graduates, faculty, and parents gathered in the gymnasium, where the temperature rose by the minute. It gets hot in South Georgia in June. The Governor began his speech, sweat dripping, with these words:

> I'll be a better man for having been here this day. If hell is any hotter than this I'm determined not to go there. If God gives me strength to get back to Atlanta, I'm going to draw on the discretionary fund and air-condition this building.

My friend told me that this was one politician who kept his word. The gym received a cooling system. The Governor may still think that everyone wore a heavy, serge gown that day!

Report by Registrar, Georgia Southwestern College (now University).

A Heroine and an Encourager

A Woman of Courage

I was the administrator of a Georgia community college, which among other enterprises had a strong nursing program. Students engaged in a pressure-packed series of courses in the classroom and clinical rotations in the hospital. After two years they received the college degree and upon completion of state board exams, the R. N. Three, five-hour courses made a standard load each quarter; clinical assignments might increase it to twenty.

The academic dean came one day with an unusual request, a student pleading to take a twenty-five-hour load. He had said "no" and the student was appealing. I concurred with his decision though he didn't seem happy about it. He asked, "Will you talk with her?" I agreed to this, though firm in my attitude. "Twenty hours, perhaps, twenty-five, never."

The student, a young black woman of perhaps thirty years of age, made a poignant plea that went something like this: "I'm the first person in my family ever to attend college. It is my dream to become a nurse. If I can't take these five courses now I'll have to wait a whole year to pick up the remainder. I must finish the program, start my profession and help support my family. My mother has promised to stay with us, do the housework and look after the children. My husband will help. All I have to do is study and I will give it my best." For the only time in my life I approved a twenty-five-hour load for a student, average in academic ability. However, she excelled in nursing courses.

The student made an all-out successful effort, and graduated in June with her family and peers applauding enthusiastically, as she received her diploma. Then the nursing director told me the rest of the story. On duty at night as a student nurse the young woman had become concerned about a patient who was not doing well. The supervising nurse said, "We are using the procedure the doctor ordered. Don't worry about it." The student protested and mentioned a new procedure for such situations, to no avail. The supervisor told her to back off. Troubled, the student made a painful decision. She broke the chain of command, called the doctor and told him the patient was in danger. The doctor came to the hospital, changed the procedure, and saved the patient's life.

Later, a staff meeting was called, this case was discussed, and policy was changed to cover such circumstances. One young black woman, willing to risk her career, had the courage to put the welfare of the individual above the system. I get an inspirational lift as I recollect this case and the nursing student who, in a crisis, demonstrated the qualities of a heroine.

Everything Is Beautiful

When we lived in Georgia we would visit beautiful Callaway Gardens often for a civic club or educational convention. We loved to eat breakfast in the great dining room of the large inn. Here country ham, grits, eggs, hot biscuits, and muscadine preserves were served. One waiter, a middle-aged black man, circulated continuously with a pitcher of hot coffee in his hand and a cheery smile on his face. Everywhere he went his message was, "Everything is beautiful. How 'bout some coffee? Everything's beautiful. Have some red-hot coffee?" He said it dozens of times during a meal. One could conclude that it was trite, or overdone. However, years later, the other servers are forgotten and I have no idea who the restaurant manager was but I remember the optimistic words of that smiling waiter. Later I learned that he had survived a terrible wreck and battled terrible pain. Yet he demonstrated his love for life by being upbeat. What a wonderful thing it would be if all of us could occasionally say, "Life is beautiful, how can I serve you? Everything is beautiful. Can I serve you some red-hot coffee?"

Mystery—The Bermuda Triangle

On December 5, 1945, five Naval torpedo bombers (TBF Avengers) left Fort Lauderdale, Florida on a training mission into the heart of the Bermuda Triangle. It was to be a 2½ hour flight. This vast stretch of the Atlantic reaches from the southern Florida coast to Puerto Rico, and thence to the Bermuda Islands about 600 miles off the Carolina Coast. The TBFs mysteriously vanished and have never been found. A Martin Mariner (PBM), sent to search for them, disappeared when twenty minutes into its flight. Twenty-seven lives were lost, in all. The Navy searched for four days, found no wreckage or survivors, closed the investigation, and described pilots and crew "lost at sea." The mystery of these losses joins a centuries-old succession of strange happenings, in this sprawling area of the Atlantic Ocean.

The term "Bermuda Triangle" was coined in 1964 and is the common one used, though some say "Devil's Triangle." Here are a few of the unexplained reported happenings in this intriguing portion of the Atlantic:

- Columbus reported strange lights and a disordered compass as he approached the Bahamas.

- *The Cyclops*, with over 300 aboard, disappeared without a trace.
- In 1980 a freighter vanished and was never found.
- In 1978 a charter plane disappeared without explanation.
- Charles Lindbergh, in 1928, the year after his transatlantic trip, on a night flight from Cuba, reported that his compass began spinning. (A phenomenon often reported in the "Devil's Triangle.") When the sun came up he discovered he was headed out to sea.
- Bruce Gernom, interviewed on television, reported that in 1974, flying toward Miami, he ran into an "electronic fog." A strange black cloud appeared before him. He entered it and found himself flying inside a tunnel. When he broke out of it, he was over Miami Beach. He flew 100 miles in three minutes and believes he entered a "time warp." Some call this a "worm hole."
- An aircraft controller in St. Thomas reported that a plane he was directing to land disappeared when it was two miles away.

The five TBFs, which vanished in December, 1945, were on a typical training mission out of Fort Lauderdale. The flight plan ordered them to fly southeast, turn north to the Bahamas, and practice bombing runs near Hen and Chicken Shoals. Then they would proceed further north, over Grand Bahama Island before turning west toward home base.

At 3:40, Flight 19 of TBFs was supposed to sight Grand Bahama but it never did. Lt. Taylor, the flight leader, reported that his compass was not working and

146

that they were lost. He thought they were over the Florida Keys, and wanted to fly northeast. Another pilot argued that they were in the Bahamas and should fly west. At 5:19 Taylor issued the order "Prepare to ditch." After this there was silence, except for a garbled radio report about 7:00.

A search plane, Martin Mariner (PBM), with thirteen men aboard, was sent to look for the torpedo bombers and soon disappeared. A tanker reported an explosion and a weird, green light, and gave the coordinates. The Navy searched this area and found an oil slick but no wreckage or survivors.

The Navy conducted the largest search since the effort to find Amelia Earhart, but to no avail. The mystery of the Bermuda Triangle is carried forward. They noted that the Gulf Stream, surging through the area, may have carried away some debris but not the huge 1-ton engines of the PBM.

The best explanation of the loss of the TBFs is that Lt. Taylor developed a kind of mental breakdown, "spatial disorientation." He was convinced he was over the Keys and flew northeast.

Human fallibility, not the mysteries of the Bermuda Triangle, explain the loss of Flight 19.

I have a personal interest in the loss of the planes. As a Navy Lt. (Jg), I was brought in a few weeks later, to the headquarters of the Gulf Sea Frontier and Seventh Naval District, as an operations officer, replacing the officer in charge when the planes disappeared. I should have asked more questions, though the Navy wasn't talking much about it. I was soon wrapped up in my duties—air-sea rescue, dealing with broken-down banana boats somewhere, arranging to get a sailor with an attack of appendicitis to a base where there was a doctor, and keeping up with all ships in the area. My orders went out signed "Lt. (Jg) Homer J. Adams, for Admiral Shafroth." This didn't impress some Captains of large ships.

In recent years the Sci-Fi T.V. Channel launched an extensive investigation to try to unravel the puzzle of the lost planes. A research team, headed by David Bright, made an underwater search, for miles around the site where the *Mariner* disappeared. They used electronic equipment, trolled underwater, and sent down divers to explore the barren ocean floor, to no avail. The explorers did experience an unusual loss of power and had to call for rescue.

Rick Siegfred, piloting a TBF, one of twelve of these World War II planes still flying, re-traced the route of Flight 19, using the same equipment, and found nothing unusual to report. One investigator, Gian Quizar, theorized that the Avengers wound up in the Okefenokee Swamp in Southern Georgia. There had been a report of five unidentified planes near Brunswick, Georgia. A search was made using satellites and "image processing," but turned up nothing. It seems to me that searching the Everglades would have made more sense.

Many have tried to explain the loss of ships, planes, and lives in the Bermuda Triangle, and the mysterious forces deemed to be at work. They include:

- It is the cosmic crossroads of space and time, related to the lost city of Atlantis.
- Waterspouts, tornadoes over the water, may be involved.
- Rogue waves, emanating from the 30,000 feet deep Puerto Rico Trench, may have destroyed ships. One such wave, seventy feet high struck a cruise ship causing injuries and damage. Hans Graeber,

at the University of Miami, studies rogue waves and thinks this explains some losses.

- One research team determined that huge gas bubbles, caused by landslides on the bottom of the ocean, could sink ships.
- Some think that AUTEC, a secret Naval facility on Andros Island, may be causing some of the phenomena, by their underwater exploration and electromagnetic testing. They have been accused of studying U.F.O.s and U.S.O.s.
- Some have theorized that the Avengers overflew the Florida Peninsula and ditched in the Gulf. Far-fetched?

My question involves variation, a force from within the globe that affects compasses. In navigation class, in midshipman school, I was taught to correct the compass starting with magnetic North, allowing for deviation, and, finally, by checking the chart for variation in the part of the ocean, before arriving at "true compass." Is it possible that extreme, uncharted variation accounts for the "spinning compass" reported by so many? I've never heard anyone comment on it.

I have a final, troubling question about the lost planes of Flight 19: Even if all five compasses were not working, why not fly west toward the setting sun? On reaching the Florida East Coast, there would be all kinds of landmarks to guide the pilots home.

As mystery writers say, "The plot thickens," and the mysteries of the past rise up to haunt us. We are likely yet to see another newspaper headline reporting some strange happening in the Bermuda Triangle.

Conversations with naval officers in the Gulf Sea Frontier operations office.
Television interviews and reports.

He Didn't Know Where He Lived

I taught a summer short course for teachers, "Methods of Teaching Social Studies," years ago. One of the topics dealt with was the use of anecdotes in teaching history, a special interest of mine. (My doctoral dissertation was on this teaching device.) I began by challenging these high school teachers to name an important person in American history and I would undertake to tell an anecdote about that individual.

Naming Lincoln caused no problem as there were many such stories. I forget which one I told. Booker T. Washington was mentioned and I gave them two. One of them linked him to Theodore Roosevelt, who helped this negro educator and orator carry his suitcases to a hotel, late one night in New York.

The anecdotes continued until someone called Richard Nixon's name, and there was a long pause. Then I had to tell them I couldn't give one. You see, part of the definition of an anecdote includes an account of "the likeable foibles of a famous personage." My understanding was that Nixon lacked likeable foibles and for that matter a sense of humor. I can recount a story told by Henry Kissinger, his Secretary of State.

He was with the President at the "Western White House" in San Clemente. Late one evening Nixon suggested to Kissinger that they take a ride to his old neighborhood. The driver was called and off they went to look for the house, in Whittier, where Nixon lived as a boy.

Up one street and down another they went, looking, in vain, for the boyhood home. He just could not remember where it was. Someone observed that this was Nixon's lifelong problem—he didn't know where he lived.

Richard Nixon was a tragic figure, a man of many talents, yet harboring a fascination with power and suspicion of enemies, to the point of paranoia. The Watergate tapes certainly revealed the dark side of the man.

President Nixon was very shy, and apparently indecisive. The President had a meeting with Henry Kissinger to discuss his becoming National Security Advisor, but did not come out and offer the position. A few days later a staff member called and asked, "Are you going to take the job?" Kissinger answered, "What job?" The answer was, "We had better start over." A few days later the President called and offered the job.

Later he was at San Clemente and the President asked him to go swimming. As they were about to leave the pool the President said, "I'm having a press conference tomorrow and I would like to announce you as the new Secretary of State." On this indirect approach Henry Kissinger accepted the prestigious position.[1]

President Nixon had two attractive daughters and a lovely wife, Pat. At a political gathering she was signing autographs while he talked with others. I loaned her a pen and tried to leave it with her. She said, "No, no, no" and insisted on returning it. She didn't want anyone saying, "I loaned Pat Nixon a pen and she didn't return it."

After President Nixon's forced resignation (public pressure and the threat of impeachment), he wrote books that revealed a wide knowledge of politics and world affairs. They helped redeem his reputation.[2]

[1] Henry Kissinger on the "Tonight Show," 4/19/94.
[2] Various news reports.

151

VI
Current

Unusual Angel

As the story of Brian Nichols and Ashley Smith unfolded on March 11, 2005, the attention of the nation was captured. Brian Nichols was on his way to court in Atlanta, Georgia to be tried on a second rape charge. He was accompanied by a single sheriff's deputy, a small, female guard. He overpowered her, escaped to the courtroom where, it is alleged, he shot a judge and court clerk and at street level, another law enforcement officer. Then he highjacked cars, and, in North Atlanta, shot another man, who happened to be a federal government official.

A massive manhunt ensued. Fast forward to Ashley Smith, a widowed mother of a five-year-old daughter, who lived alone in an apartment Northeast of Atlanta. In the early hours of the morning she drove to a convenience store for cigarettes. On her return, about 2:30 A.M., she was taken captive by Brian Nichols, killer on the run. He took her to her apartment and held her hostage for seven hours, bound by duct tape and electric cord, part of the time.

The story of her captivity, told in the press, in television interviews, and in her book, *Unlikely Angel*, is an enthralling account of the criminal mind, and the resolute spirit of a young woman, battered by life, but struggling upward. How she survived this frightening experience without bodily harm, and called 911 to report Nichol's location, is a tribute to her clear thinking, courage, and faith in God.

Ashley seemed to have instinctively done all the right things, techniques taught to hostage negotiators. She kept her poise, treated Nichols as a human being, empathized with him and his predicament, won his confidence, revealed her troubled past, and opened the door of hope. At about 4:00 A.M. she began to talk with him about giving himself up. They turned on the T. V. and saw a report of Deputy Hall whom he had injured. He looked up and said, "God forgive me. Please let her live." He seemed especially touched that Ashley would cook breakfast for him.

At one point she asked if she could read, and the volume was Rick Warren's book, *The Purpose Driven Life*. He agreed to this and then, later, asked her to read aloud. She read to him Chapter 5, "Using What God Gave Me." From this reading and further conversation she implanted the idea that there still could be purpose and meaning in his life.

She apparently gained his sympathy by telling about her daughter, taken away from her by the Court, and living with her parents in Augusta, Georgia. He permitted her to leave knowing she planned to drive to Augusta. His last words to here were, "Tell your daughter 'Hi' for me."

Nichols seemed to know that Ashley would call the police. She did and they were slow to be convinced that she was telling the truth. Finally they swung into action and SWAT teams surrounded the apartment complex.

They expected resistance but Nichols slowly walked out, waving a white towel. He was indicted on fifty-four counts.

On Fox News, 10/4/05, she answered the question as to why Nichols chose that apartment complex and took her hostage, by saying, "God was in it." She went on to say that the whole ordeal was a life-changing experience. She said that "it was a turning point," and that she "returned to God," and that she has not used drugs since.

Ashley has received $70,000 in rewards and has had numerous offers of speaking engagements, books, and movies. She says that she will give a portion of the proceeds from her forthcoming book to families of the victims.

The Tennessean, 9/28/01.
Fox News, 10/7/05.
Numerous media reports.

Historical One-liners

History consists of complex accounts and simple stories but history often consists of a single powerful statement—a one-liner, if you please. Of course one needs a little background to fully appreciate the pointed statement. Here are some one-liners, those underlined, and each one illustrating a point.

Sir Walter Raleigh, a favorite of Queen Elizabeth, earned the ire of James I who accused him of trying to supplant James I with his cousin, Arabella Stuart. He was imprisoned for years but was released to go on a gold-hunting mission in Spanish America. Though this expedition failed, it angered the Spanish. Thus to placate Spain he was executed. Courtly to the last he tested the headsman's axe and said *"This is sharp medicine but it cures all ills."*[1]

The signing of the Declaration of Independence on August 2, 1776, was a solemn event. John Hancock, as President of Congress, signed first and observed that they must all hang together. Rarely at a loss for a quip, Franklin responded, *"Yes, we must all hang together, or most assuredly we must all hang separately."*[2]

During the Revolutionary War, Ethan Allen and his "Green Mountain Boys" attacked the British in Fort Ticonderoga. Responding to a call to surrender, the British general shouted, "In whose name do you make this demand?" The doughty American answered, *"In the name of the Lord God Jehovah and the Continental Congress."* The British surrendered.

In 1787 delegates were chosen to attend a national convention to amend and improve the "Articles of Confederation," under which Americans were governed. The delegates went beyond their charter, immediately scrapped the "Articles" and started to write the Constitution. The canny Patrick Henry had refused to be a delegate, saying, *"I smelt a rat."* The Articles of Confederation was weak but it was all the Americans would tolerate in 1781 and it served as a stepping stone to constitutional government.

Texans fought Mexico in the "Battle of San Jacinto" in 1836. They swept into battle (which they won) to the tune the band was playing, *"Come to the bower I have shaded for you."*

John Adams lay dying on July 4, 1826. His thoughts turned to his friend and former colleague, and he said, *"Thomas Jefferson survives. Independence forever."* He did not know that Jefferson died the same day, his last words being, *"Is it the fourth? I resign my spirit to God."*

The United States came into World War I after France and other allies had been fighting Germany for three years. Victory seemed remote. Then the U.S. entered the war. An officer, landing in France with the first American troops, seized the historic moment, and declaimed, *"Lafayette, we are here."*

It was 1933 and the Great Depression was on. Thousands of banks closed, the stock exchange shut down. Twenty-five percent of people were out of work, some were destitute and normal times a distant hope. Then came Franklin D. Roosevelt, recently elected President, and saying, *"The only thing we have to fear is fear itself."*

People began to take courage. Then he began his "fireside chats" over the radio. Millions of Americans heard that resonant tenor voice speaking assurance and confidence and were encouraged. Banks began to reopen, as well as the stock exchange, and the "New Deal" programs to get money into the hands of consumers were started. Then Depression lasted for years but people started looking up in 1933.[3]

It is interesting to note that the two Roosevelts, FDR and T.R., are the only ones called by their initials.

President Franklin D. Roosevelt was asked to address the annual meeting of the "Daughters of the American Revolution." His opening statement was, *Fellow Immigrants.* The shocked ladies, proud of their ancestry, were hard put to complain for the Roosevelts had been in the Hudson River Valley since the 1600s.

Sam Rayburn chaired more than one Democratic convention. He moved business right along. One party member complained that those who opposed the motion didn't have a chance to express it. Rayburn explained it by saying, *"You lose a lot of good motions if you put the negative side of the question."*

An old twentieth century pro, "Tip" O'Neill, seasoned by many a political struggle, made a statement, oft quoted for many years, *"All politics is local."*

[1] Churchill, Winston, *The New World*, Dodd, Mead and Company, New York, 1956. Churchill did not include the last statement.
[2] Bailey, Thomas A., Kennedy, David M., *The American Pageant*, Ninth Edition, Lexington, Mass, D. C. Heath and Co., 1991.
[3] Various secondary sources.

American Presidents

Presidents of the United States, severally and as a group, hold great interest to Americans. Here are some intriguing samples of information, truths not generally known.[1]

Collectively Viewed

- Twelve presidents were generals before taking office.
- Nine presidents did not attend college.
- To be a "great" president seems to require a "great" crisis. Lincoln and F. D. R. had their share. Historians don't characterize presidents as "good" or "bad" but on strength of leadership and the extent to which they enlarged the president's office. They refer to presidents as "great," "near great," "average," or "failure."
- Two men have been elected president while in the Senate—Harding and Kennedy.
- What presidents do after their terms are over, captures public attention. Some stay active in politics, others write books, or make speeches at home or abroad for huge fees. Others, like Jimmy Carter, give their energies to good works and humanitarian enterprises.
- Several made notable contributions in different government careers—John Quincy Adams in the House of Representatives, Andrew Johnson in the Senate (alongside those who had tried to remove him from office) and Taft on the Supreme Court. Two men ran again years later, Grant, in 1880, and T. Roosevelt in 1912. Both lost.
- Some presidents surprise everyone by acting differently than expected. Andrew Johnson came into office breathing fire and slaughter. Some Radical Republicans feared he would start hanging Confederates. Instead, he adopted Lincoln's moderate plan of reconstruction for restoration of Confederate states and amnesty for most of the military.

- Three men occupied the White House in 1881—Hayes, Garfield, and Arthur.
- Chester Arthur was a classic example of the spoils system, representing the corrupt New York political ring. He turned out to be a civil service reformer, signing the Pendleton Act in 1883.
- Gerald Ford served as Vice-President and President, though not elected to either position.

Little Known Truths about Presidents

- Which president gave an interview from the Potomac? John Quincy Adams liked to swim in the river early in the morning. An indomitable reporter, Anne Royall, tracked him down, sat on his clothes on the bank, and demanded that he answer her questions. He did, while chest-deep in water.
- Who was the youngest man elected president? Grant, at 46; Kennedy, later, at 43.
- Which president changed his name? Hiram Ulysses Grant showed up at West Point and was mistakenly checked in as Ulysses S. Grant. He noticed the discrepancy but didn't bother to change it. He was U.S. Grant from then on.
- What president won a horse and carriage race? Grant did and also got a speeding ticket for riding his horse too fast.
- What president was elected but didn't know it until weeks later? Hayes was late getting the word.
- Who was a preacher and a college president before being president? James A. Garfield, who impressed educators with the statement that a student on one end of a log and Mark Hopkins on the other was a college.

- Which president had the shortest work day? Chester Arthur would stroll into the office at 10:00 and leave at 4:00, but he got a lot of work done.
- Which president refused to serve alcoholic beverages in the White House? This was Rutherford Hayes and his wife was disrespectfully called "Lemonade Lucy."
- What presidential candidate was shot but refused to fall? T. Roosevelt running on the "Bull Moose" ticket in 1912, was shot, said "I have a bullet in my body," finished his speech and then went to the hospital. This impressed the public but not enough to elect him.
- What president was elected in a campaign with a shared political slogan? In 1884, referring to Cleveland's illegitimate child, the Republicans would chant "Ma, Ma, where's my Pa?" The Democrats would answer, "Off to the White House, ha, ha, ha."
- Did a grandfather and grandson serve as president? Yes, William Henry, and Benjamin Harrison.
- Which president "sat out" a term? Cleveland failed to get re-elected in 1888 but tried again in 1892 and won.
- Who first had electricity put in the White House? The Harrisons, but they were afraid to touch the switch!
- Who was the first president to get married in the White House? Cleveland, a 47-year-old man married a 20-year-old woman.
- Which was the only president to hold the Ph.D. degree? Wilson, a former political science professor.

- Which president had his picture on the $100,000 bill? Wilson, though the bill was never circulated. It was used by the Federal Reserve and the Treasury Department.
- Which president was sworn in by a Justice of the Peace? Calvin Coolidge, after the death of President Harding. His father, a Justice of the Peace, swore him in by lamp light, in a Vermont farmhouse.
- Which president was a reckless gambler? W. G. Harding had poker games at the White House and once gambled away a set of presidential china from the Harrison administration.
- Which president made the toughest decision? Harry Truman made the fateful decision to drop the atomic bomb in August, 1945.
- Which president was forced to resign? Nixon did in 1974, thereby avoiding impeachment.
- Which president was kicked out of his party? Tyler angered his fellow Whigs by his presidential policies and they read him out of the party. He served out his term as a man without a party.
- Which president made sure the White House had milk? William Henry Harrison. When he moved into the White House he went to the market and bought a cow. The seller helped him drive the cow home and was astonished when they approached the destination.
- Which President strongly opposed racial prejudice in athletics? Gerald R. Ford. When Gerald Ford was the Center and Captain of the University of Michigan football team, Georgia Tech came to town to play. They discovered a black player on

Ford's team and refused to play unless he was removed from the game. Ford was furious over the racial prejudice and the University caving in to it. He protested and announced that he would not play. Only when his black team mate urged him to play did he agree to do so.[2]

United States presidents were real, live people with their foibles, prejudices, and strengths. Some had clay feet, and strayed grievously. This was sometimes hushed, gleefully reported in other cases. Even so, the presidents have helped shape the course of the nation.

[1] Many books, lectures by history professors and the TV series *The Presidents* on the History Channel, July 1, 2006.
[2] Tom Brokaw at President Ford's funeral, January 2, 2007.

Our Language Changes

The history of the English Language is an interesting topic to pursue. To watch and hear history in the making is fascinating. The way Americans talk is constantly changing. Let's look at some patterns of speech that have emerged in recent years.

Changes

From	To
All the time . . .	Twenty-four seven
You're welcome	No problem
Go to the extreme	Push the envelope
Chickens come home to roost	What goes around comes around
I understand	My sense is
Good response	Resonates well
Great!	Cool!
He has a bad attitude	He has an attitude
In agreement	Singing off the same page
Like father; like son	The nut doesn't fall far from the tree
Unnecessary instruction	Preaching to the choir
Accept responsibility	Step up
Satisfactory	Perfect
That's outstanding	Awesome
Resources	Assets
Military presence	Boots on the ground

The Search for Political Correctness

Americans are finding new terms often not as accurate as the ones they replace, but with a softer effect. Examples are:

Physically challenged for disabled.
Horizontally challenged for overweight.
Vertically challenged for short.
Outsourced for fired.
And from the world of spies and terrorism, the chilling phrase, "Terminated with extreme prejudice," meaning killed.

Redundancy

Americans, especially the educated ones, have a passion for piling unnecessary words on top of words. It is called redundancy. This usually occurs with the spoken word, as proofreaders edit these out of print. Retired, and interested in world events, I watch a lot of TV, especially news. I am appalled at the way news commentators, CEOs, and government leaders resort to redundance. I have made a list of these heard in recent years and they number 230. Here are some examples of needless repetition, with comment:

- Chances are nil to none (also slim).
- Give back in return (said by a spokesman for the Mayor of New York).
- Currently in effect (stated by a Justice Department spokesman).
- In the next few days to come (a T.V. weatherman said it).
- Mental deliberations (spoken by a lawyer who is also a psychiatrist).
- At this time as we speak (said by my favorite TV weatherman).
- Not necessarily necessary (spoken by a cabinet member, the one on TV a lot).
- Self indulge itself (so stated a Supreme Court Justice in an official document).
- Walked on foot (spoken by John Walker Lindh who worked for the Taliban).
- Visibly displayed (better than invisibly displayed).
- Trained professional (What a relief to find that he was not an amateur professional!).

Americans can't change history but we can change history in the making by choosing clear, simple language over the verbose.

Source: This material comes from newspapers and magazines, observation of T.V. news and taking notes over a period of several years.

University Faculty and Presidents

General Dwight Eisenhower retired from the army and became President of Columbia University. Speaking to the assembled faculty and unaccustomed to the protocol of academe, he referred to the faculty as "You employees of the University." Shock prevailed. Then a senior professor stood and said, "Mr. President, we are not employees of the University; we _are_ the University."

This reminds me of the response to a college president who used the term, "my faculty." A professor, speaking for his colleagues said, "You are our president but we are not your faculty!"

College administrators also comment, as, "Faculty are those who think otherwise."

Someone said "The Dean represents the faculty to the President and the President to the faculty." Another put it this way—"The President is the shepherd of the academic flock; the Dean is the crook at the head of the staff." There is a creative tension between faculty and administration, as I learned from years spent on both sides of the fence.

Faculty do not have authority upward, but they have influence and they can hasten the departure of the President or Chancellor. The President of the University of California, Clark Kerr, may have undertaken too much change, and left as he said, "The same way I came, fired with enthusiasm."

President Summers, of Harvard, angered the faculty by making a remark about women having less ability than men in certain areas. This may be true just as women are stronger than men in others. However, it was not politically correct to say it even if it was part of a scholarly study. This able administrator had to leave, despite impressive accomplishments.

I once had a department head who told me, "My department is doing more work and bringing in more money for this college than all your overpaid deans put together." He and his instructors were doing excellent work, so I tolerated his pointed remarks, laughed, and moved on.

All this leads to a bit of humor about the "groves of academe." A university professor prayed, "Oh, Lord, deliver me from intellectual arrogance, which, for your information, is defined in the following terms . . . "

Source: Various magazines and information garnered at professional education meetings.

Unusual Students I Have Known

The fascinating thing about social history is its flexibility. It stretches to cover all sorts of actions, attitudes, and interests of a bygone era. Writers like Mark Sullivan and Frederick Allen wrote about a wide variety of interests, including advertising and fashions early in the Twentieth Century. This opens the door for me to write about college students and the way they act.

I taught social studies in high school for six years and history in college for fourteen years before going into administration for twenty-four years.

Thinking of the thousands in my classes some of which were sixty or seventy in size, I find that certain individuals, or categories, stand out. Here are descriptions of some.

One category is the housewives who return to college after their children are in school. They come fearfully, doubting that they can compete with bright young sophomores with educational momentum going. They don't realize what they have going for them—wisdom from life's experiences, tremendous motivation and a wonderful work ethic. They earn top grades and walk away with high honors at graduation. It's still about the same as it was forty years ago. Attend a university graduation and note that when the "magna cum laude" graduate marches across the stage, it will often be a mature person. Here are others.

The superb achiever. I had two students Jerry and John, older than the other students, whose answers on essay questions were like term papers. They must have out-guessed me on which questions I would ask and practiced in advance! I learned a lot of history from their research papers.

The overachiever. Jack enrolled in my one-hour reading and research course. I had set reasonable minimum reading and reporting requirements. He turned in one report of 100 typewritten pages!

All my courses required extra reading, say 500–1,000 pages for the quarter. More than once I've gone into a lower division history course and held up William Shirer's *The Rise and Fall of the Third Reich* (1200 pages) and say "There may be one person in this college, or even in this class, who would read this massive classic work and report on it." Often one would.

The earnest student. This one says, "Can I do some extra work to pull up my grade?" Indeed they could.

The unrealistic student. The top student in one class told me, "I hate to read." And he planned to be a history teacher! I explained the realities of graduate school and expectations of the students' reading.

The pleader. This student thinks that grades are given on the basis of need, which he or she will eloquently, even tearfully describe.

The debater. This student challenges the grade arguing that it should be higher, and somehow is not quite fair. My answer is "Here is the formula and the range and the record of all your tests, pop quizzes, and term paper. Figure your own grade. It is simple mathematics." Debate usually ends here. The only thing worse is a parent calling, and issuing the arguments. It doesn't happen often.

The creative student. It was 1957 and the crisis was on in Little Rock over admitting blacks to formerly all-white high schools. The Governor was fulminating, and federal troops were called out. In my classes we always stopped what we were doing to discuss history in the making. One student was absent and I got a card from him saying, "I'm out here in Little Rock (360 miles away) studying the crisis, close-up." You can be sure we heard his report when he returned.

The young scholar. I was teaching an American History course for the University of Tennessee at Sewart Air Force Base. Civilians were also allowed to register. One brought his ten year-old son with him one evening. The lad was a history buff. During the lecture I said something, in passing, about General Lee being involved in the First Battle of Bull Run. At the mid-evening break little Jonathan approached me and said, "I thought General Lee was in Western Virginia in July of 1861." Mental wheels turned and I responded, "You are exactly right." When class began I made the correction and gave the boy the credit. Forty years later he still has an avid interest in Civil War history.

The average student. She was an elementary education major and struggled to get her grades high enough to graduate. I probably advised her to repeat a course so the latter, with a higher grade would improve her G.P.A. But she proved to be an excellent teacher. She had creativity, compassion, and dedication. She earned such a reputation that her Alma Mater called her back to instruct other teachers in summer school courses. There are hundreds out there like her.

The apocryphal student. This could have happened but I can't prove it. A student attended class two days, dropped out, returned to take the final exam and made 96. The teacher wondered how this could be. The student said, "I would have made 100, but you said something that second day that confused me." Let the reader be the judge.

Teaching is a wonderful profession. I appreciated all my students and tried to make history interesting for them. It is very satisfying to hear a former student say, years later, "You made history come alive for me." They didn't say it was easy but they did imply that the life and sparkle of history had been revealed.

100 Favorite Stories

(Selections)

I have been gathering humor materials for thirty years and have a book, written up piecemeal, entitled *A Study of Humor*. One of these days it will be finished. One chapter is named "My 100 Favorite Stories." Here are a few of them. Some are true, others could be true and some should be labeled "unlikely." Good social history includes a discussion of what people thought was funny in a certain era.

Anxious to Please

A man was bad to drink and came home late one night, really under the weather. Fumbling with the door, he couldn't get the key in the lock. His wife flung the door open and he sprawled inside. She lit in on him, and then demanded, "What do you have to say for yourself?"

Looking up he said, "I don't have a prepared statement but I'm willing to take questions from the floor!"

Husband and Wife

A man and his wife had argued and were driving along, pouting. Seeing a mule in a field the husband asked, "Is that mule one of your relatives?" She answered, "Yes, he's related by marriage."

Lucky Golfer

A golfer was on the course near a highway. He took a mighty swing, hooked the ball, and watched it head toward a passing Greyhound bus. It bounced off a hub-cap, came back on the green and went into the hole. His friend asked, "How in the world did you do that?" The golfer answered, "It helps to know the bus schedule."

Wrong Way

A lady realized that her husband stopped by his favorite watering hole after work and, concerned about his safety, called him on his cell phone. She said, "I just heard on the radio, that there is a crazy man driving the wrong way on the interstate. Be careful." He answered, "You're wrong; there are hundreds of people driving the wrong way!"

New Diet

A new diet permits you to eat three big meals a day and a bedtime snack, but you must eat a slice of onion and a clove of garlic at each meal.

You won't lose weight but you'll look smaller from a distance.

Shingles

A man came into a doctor's office and said to the receptionist, "I've got shingles." She told him to have a seat. Twenty minutes later she took him to a room and asked him to wait. A nurse came in and asked why he was there. He said, "I've got shingles." She said, "Wait here." Twenty minutes later a doctor came in and said, "What have you got?" He said, "I've got shingles and I need someone to help me unload them from the truck."

Three Doctors

Three doctors came to heaven's gate and were questioned by St. Peter. The first doctor was asked to identify himself. He said, "I'm a doctor who served as a medical missionary in Africa." St. Peter said, "Come right in." The next one said, "I ran a clinic in the inner city." And the answer was, "Come right in." The third doctor said, "I ran an HMO on earth." St. Peter said, "You can enter, but you can only stay 3 days."

Honest Answers

A tourist missed his road and wound up in the hills. Spying an old gentleman in a garden he "hollered," "How do you get to town?" The answer came back: "Usually my son-in-law takes me."

She Said "Yes"

A widow and widower started going out for coffee (de-caf). He proposed and she quickly said "yes." He slept well that night, awoke, and tried to remember her answer. He called and asked her what it was. She answered, "Of course I said 'yes,' but I'm so glad you called. I couldn't remember who proposed."

Grandmothers

A Grandmother sat on the beach with her grandson. He had his little sunsuit, bucket and shovel. A big wave came and took him out to sea. "Oh Lord," she prayed, "Save my grandson." Immediately, a wave brought him back—sunsuit, bucket and all. She cupped her hands, looked to heaven, and yelled, "He had a hat."

Up the Paddle

A man paddled his canoe upstream several miles in a small stream. He developed a terrible catch in his back and couldn't straighten up. What to do? He thrust his paddle into the water and touched bottom. Then he moved hand over hand up the handle, straightening a little with each move. Finally he stepped out of the canoe, standing straight. He was up the paddle without a crick.

Wild Pig

My family has a reunion each July in the Southern farm community where we grew up. My grandfather Adams had ten children and they in turn had sizable families. There were fifty of us first cousins so reunions were lively.

During the weekend at one reunion, my cousin Bradberry and I were on the back porch of Uncle Eddie's farmhouse, cranking a freezer of ice cream. An interesting drama unfolded. A tenant family, husband and wife and two boys, were trying to head a large pig through a gate and into the barnyard. He didn't want to go and got more excited as they yelled and waved their arms, while she flapped her apron.

Tension mounted and the shoat (adolescent pig) made a mad dash to break through the circle. He charged toward the woman. As he approached she extended her arms and spread her legs. The squealing porker ran between her legs, her dress tightened and the pig was stuck. He had momentum and kept moving. All of us viewed the amazing scene—a woman riding a pig backward! The woman screamed, the boys laughed, the father gave them a sour look, and we choked back the merriment. She must have ridden ten or fifteen feet before falling off.

The pig was finally corralled. The scene was cleared and we let loose gales of laughter. I thought my cousin would roll on the floor. For years after that he would ask me, "Do you remember the woman riding the pig?"

Hurricane Katrina

During the week of August 22, 2005, Katrina swept out of the Caribbean, lashed Key West, whirled its way north, gaining power, changing to Category 5, and struck, with devastating force, Louisiana, Mississippi, and Alabama on Monday, August 29. The worst of the wind was east of New Orleans and citizens of that city, for a few hours, thought they had dodged the bullet. Then the levees, protecting this below sea level city broke, and 80 percent of New Orleans was flooded. Water, perhaps five feet deep on the average, was fifteen feet deep in other areas. About 100,000 people were stranded, and many perished, on the second floors of their houses or on the rooftops.

Tuesday, Wednesday, and Thursday passed without significant relief and rescue efforts occurring. People perched on roofs and bridges, with 25,000 gathered in the Superdome, and 10,000 in the Convention Center. Chaos reigned, looters were active, and members of the over-worked police force began to disappear, 249 in all. A New Orleans TV station reported a woman wading down the street pushing her husband's body on a door.

At the Convention Center medical problems abounded. Dr. Greg Henderson arrived there on Friday, the only doctor for 10,000 people. They were stacking the dead on the second floor. People were having seizures, some needed dialysis and couldn't get it, and all manner of disease was present.

At the Superdome, 25,000 people suffered for four days in a humid environment with little food and water, and toilets not working. Some died, including one man who committed suicide.

Law and order in the city failed and looters were active, about 3,000 of them. They consisted of poor people, desperate for food and water, greedy lawbreakers seizing guns, jewelry, and TV sets, and hardened criminals coming, like vultures, from all over the country. Police had to escort a doctor, taking drugs to a clinic.

Relief supplies, millions of meals ready to eat (MRE), fleets of trucks hauling water and ice, and security forces which should have started to come on Tuesday arrived in force on Friday and on following days. The blame game started early in the week and there was plenty to go around. The Mayor didn't use dozens of available busses to evacuate people, the Governor was slow to send National Guard troops, and FEMA, which had drilled for years for such catastrophes, seemed paralyzed. There were accusations of race discrimination but it would seem that government ineptness was color blind.

Then the tide turned and evacuees were taken to cities all over the United States. Houston, Texas accepted 250,000 homeless. A church in Atlanta took in nine refugees, called them down front in a service, and the pastor gave each a key to an automobile and a key to a house. Heroes were found on every side—doctors and medical staff who worked night and day under horrendous conditions, people in boats and helicopters who risked their lives to rescue those in distress, and many more.

Never was there such an outpouring of concern and compassion from the American people. Within three weeks Americans gave over a billion dollars and half a billion dollars had been given the Red Cross. Volunteers and mountains of supplies poured into the stricken area from all sides.

Unlike the 9/11 disaster, New Orleans and the rest of the Gulf were adequately warned of a possible catastrophe. Detailed reports and newspaper articles predicting disaster were available and a computer model showed broken levees and a flooded New Orleans. Foresight was 20/20; the will to act was lacking. In 1997 Congress gave FEMA $500,000 to develop a comprehensive plan to evacuate New Orleans. This money was turned over to the State of Louisiana which used it to study the building of a new bridge.

There was a day when partisan bickering and accusations would have been delayed until the hurricane was over, destruction analyzed, and the bodies counted. Not so this time. The Democrats blamed the Bush administration for relief and rescue efforts being too little, and too late, and providing insufficient security forces. Many Americans, including evacuees, spread blame all up and down the line, including the New Orleans Mayor and the Louisiana Governor.

As a new, Category 4 Hurricane, Rita, approached the Gulf coast on September 23, water overrode the patched levees and New Orleans, which had been pumped dry, was flooded again. The merciless hurricane Katrina left 1,119 dead and damages totaling a possible $200 billion.

Several political results of Katrina are visible. The G.O.P. plans to cut taxes and overhaul Social Security are off the table. The $62 billion for relief and rebuilding, already voted by Congress, may soar to $200 billion. How this will be spent and what offsets will be required is bound to produce political controversy for years to come.

A Senate Committee chaired by Senator Collins completed an eight-month study and concludes that FEMA is hopelessly weak and disorganized and dysfunctional. It ought to be dissolved and be replaced with a new organization, within the Homeland Defense Department.

Dozens of T.V. reports, newspapers, and news magazines.

Epilogue

Looking back at the stories, I asked myself, "Do they constitute social history or should they be described as political, military, or economic history? What about biography?" The answer that emerged was "All of the above."

I've also asked myself, "What if an editor wanted another twenty-five stories?" My answer is, "It can be done, but it will take a few months." There are many more stories out there.

In some college history classes or in seminars for social studies teachers, I have dared to say "Name some character in American history and I will undertake to tell you an anecdote about that person." They loved it! Of course there was a problem when Abraham Lincoln was named. You have to choose from a dozen good stories about him.

My regard for anecdotes and the human interest side of history stemmed from the observation that my favorite teachers were those that told the best stories. Those same professors also taught good, solid history. I had one professor who didn't use illustrations and whose speech was halting but his sheer mastery of the subject was an inspiration to me.

The use of anecdotes and humor in teaching in high school and college for many years had a favorable reaction. Dozens of former students have told me, in effect, "You made history come alive for me." They didn't say it was easy, but rather that it was interesting.

It is hoped that these brief historical accounts will add to the reader's knowledge of past events and the way people lived, and quicken an interest in the fascinating stories of the past.

About the Author

Homer J. Adams has lived in a number of different states throughout his life, including Alabama, Florida, Georgia, Ohio, and Tennessee, where he currently lives with his wife. His own college career was interrupted by a three-year tour in the Navy. After returning from the Southwest Pacific, Dr. Adams graduated from college and went on to graduate school, a move he financed by teaching high school history. Before retiring, the author served as a dean at Trevecca College in Tennessee and DeKalb College in Georgia, as well as president of Trevecca College, now Trevecca Nazarene University. He has published several books and magazine articles.